Ship of Strangers

Bob Shaw was born in Belfast in 1931 and had a technical education
which led to several years' work in structural design offices in Ireland,
England and Canada. At the age of twenty-seven he escaped into public
relations. Since then he has worked as a journalist, a full-time author and
as press officer for an aircraft firm. Married with three children, Bob
Shaw's hobbies – apart from writing – are reading, crafts, and 'sitting
with my feet up while drinking beer and yarning with kindred spirits'. He
sold his first science fiction story to the *New York Post* when he was
nineteen, and is now the author of several novels and many short stories.
His books include *The Two-Timers*, *Other Days, Other Eyes*, *The Palace of
Eternity*, *One Million Tomorrows*, *Tomorrow Lies in Ambush* and *Orbitsville*
which won the British Science Fiction Award for the best novel of 1975 –
all published in Pan.

Previously published by
Bob Shaw in Pan Books

The Two-timers
The Palace of Eternity
One Million Tomorrows
Other Days, Other Eyes
Tomorrow Lies in Ambush
Orbitsville
Cosmic Kaleidoscope
A Wreath of Stars
Medusa's Children
Who Goes Here?

Bob Shaw

Ship of Strangers

Pan Books London and Sydney

Portions of this novel have previously appeared,
in substantially different form, in *Analog*, *If* and *Universe*.

First published 1978 by Victor Gollancz Ltd
This edition published 1979 by Pan Books Ltd,
Cavaye Place, London SW10 9PG
© Bob Shaw 1978
ISBN 0 330 25661 0
Made and printed in Great Britain by
Cox & Wyman Ltd, London, Reading and Fakenham

to A. E. van Vogt,
pioneer of many trails

The untented Kosmos my abode,
  I pass, a wilful stranger;
My mistress still the open road,
  And the bright eyes of danger.

R. L. Stevenson

one

Candar waited seven thousand years before he saw his second space-ship.

He had been little more than a cub when he saw the first, but the images of that event were still bright and sharp in his memory. It had been a warm, moist morning and his mother and father had just begun cutting through a village of the two-legged food creatures. Candar was quietly watching their great grey bodies at work when his long-range senses warned him he was being approached by something very large, something which was outside all his previous experience. He raised his head, alarmed, but his parents – their perceptions swamped by the abundance of red-reeking food – remained unaware of the menace until it came into view.

The ship came in low, and was travelling so fast that the damp air was compressed into opaque grey clouds inside the shock waves created by its blunt nose. The clouds swirled around it like a tattered cloak, so that the ship skipped in and out of visibility, and Candar wondered how anything could move at such a speed and not make any sound. For a moment he was entranced by the realization that the universe contained beings whose powers were equal to, or perhaps greater than, those of his own kind.

It was not until after the big ship had passed overhead that the awful sound of it came hammering down, levelling the food creatures' flimsy huts even more efficiently than mother and father could have done. The ship banked sharply, halted high in the morning air, and suddenly Candar and his parents were lifted into the sky. Candar found that he was caught in some kind of force net. He measured its shifting frequencies, wave lengths, intensity gradients, and even discovered that his brain could produce a similar field of its own – but he could not break free of the invisible constraints which had clamped around his body.

He and his parents were swept upwards to where the sky turned black and Candar could hear the stars. The sun rapidly grew larger and then, some time later, his mother and father were released. They dwindled out of sight in a few seconds and Candar, already adapting to the strange new environment, deduced that they had been steered into a course which terminated in the sun's bright furnace. Judging by their frantic struggles as they shrank into the distance, his mother and father had performed the same calculation.

Candar dismissed them from his thoughts and tried to anticipate his own fate. There were many sentient beings within the ship, with life-glows not greatly different from those of the food creatures, but they were too remote and too well screened for him to exert any influence on their actions. He ceased the futile twisting and flailing of his body as the sun began to grow smaller. As it became just another star, and eventually faded away altogether, time ceased to have any meaning for Candar.

He remained quiescent until he perceived that a double star was brightening and apparently expelling all others from its vicinity. It blossomed and became two egg-shaped suns courting each other in binary ritual. The ship located a planet of black rock which wobbled in a precarious and highly elliptical orbit between the suns. There, far above the barren surface, it released Candar from its grip. Only by converting his body into skeins of organic rope did he survive the fall. And by the time he had reformed his sense organs the ship was gone.

Candar knew that he had been imprisoned. He also knew that on this world which could carry no trace of food he would eventually die, and there was nothing he could do but wait for that unthinkable event to take place.

His new world made its painful run between the two suns every year. Each time it did so the black rock melted and flowed like mud, and nothing survived unchanged except Candar.

And it was seven thousand years before he saw his second space-ship.

The thing Dave Surgenor detested most about high-gravity planets was the speed at which beads of sweat could move. A trickle of perspiration could form on the brow and, with a rush like that of an attacking insect, be down the side of his face and under his collar before he could raise a hand to defend himself. In his sixteen years of survey work he had never become used to it.

'If this wasn't my last trip,' Surgenor said quietly, dabbing his neck, 'I'd refuse to do any more.'

'Can I have time to think about the logic of that one?' Victor

Voysey, who was on his second mapping expedition, kept his eyes on the survey module's controls. The forward view plate, as it had done for days, showed nothing more than ripple patterns of sterile igneous rock unfolding before the vehicle's headlight, but Voysey stared at it like a tourist on an exotic pleasure cruise.

'You've *got* time to think about it,' Surgenor said. 'That's what you get most of in this job – time to sit on your backside and twiddle your thumbs and think about things. Mainly you try to think of some reason for not quitting the job the first chance you get – and that's a nice exercise in ingenuity.'

'Money.' Voysey was trying to sound cynical. 'That's why everybody signs on. And stays on.'

'It isn't worth it.'

'I'll agree with you when I've made a bundle like yours.'

Surgenor shook his head. 'You're making a terrible mistake, Victor. You're trading your life – the only one they issue you with – for money, for the privilege of altering the positions of a few electrons in a credit computer, and it's a bad deal, Victor. No matter how much money you make you'll never be able to buy this time back again.'

'The trouble with you, Dave, is that you're getting . . .' Voysey hesitated and tried to wrestle the sentence on to a new track '. . . getting that you can't remember what it's like to need money.'

Getting old, Surgenor concluded on his partner's behalf, and decided to talk about something else.

'I'll make you a side bet, ten creds to your single, that we see the ship from the top of this rise.'

'Already!' Voysey, ignoring the proposed wager, leaned forward and started tapping buttons on the range finder panel.

Surgenor, smiling a little at the younger man's excitement, rearranged his limbs on the cushioned seat and tried to make himself comfortable. It seemed like centuries since the mother ship had set its six survey modules down at the black planet's south pole and then had ghosted back into the sky to do a half circuit and land at the north pole. The ship would have completed the journey in less than an hour – the men in the modules had had to sweat it out under three gravities for twelve days as their machines zigzagged along the planet's surface. Had there been an atmosphere they could have switched to ground-effect suspension and travelled twice as fast, but this planet – one of the least hospitable Surgenor had ever seen – made no concessions of any kind to unwanted visitors.

The survey module reached the top of the crest and the horizon, which was the line separating starry blackness from dead blackness, dropped away in front. Surgenor saw the clustered lights of the mother ship, the *Sarafand*, down on the plain about ten kilometres from him.

'You were right, Dave,' Voysey said, and Surgenor repressed a grin at the note of respect in his voice. 'I think we're going to be first back, too. I don't see any other lights.'

Surgenor nodded as he scanned the pool of night, looking for the wandering glow-worms which would have represented other returning vehicles. Strictly speaking, all six modules should have been exactly the same distance out from the *Sarafand* in their respective directions, ranged in a perfect circle. During the greater part of the journey the vehicles had adhered rigidly to the survey pattern so that the data they were transmitting to the mother ship always reached it from six equally distant, equally spaced points. Any deviation from the pattern would have caused distortions in the planetary maps being built in the ship's computer deck. But each module had a minimum awareness radius of five hundred kilometres, with the result that when they got to within that distance of the mother ship the remaining territory had already been mapped six times over, and the job was well and truly finished. It was an unofficial tradition that the last five-hundred-kilometre leg of a survey was an out-and-out race for home, with champagne for the winners and appropriate salary deductions for the others.

Module Five, which was Surgenor's vehicle, had just skirted a low but jagged range of peaks and he guessed that at least two of the others would have been forced to go over the top and lose time. Somehow, in spite of all the years and light-years, he felt a renewal of the competitive urge. It could be pleasant, if not altogether appropriate, to finish his career in the Cartographical Service with a champagne toast.

'Here we go,' Voysey said as the vehicle gathered speed on the downward slope. 'A shower, a shave and champagne – what more could you ask for?'

'Well, even if we stick to the alliteration, and decide to omit vulgarities,' Surgenor replied, 'there's steak, sex, sleep . . .'

He stopped speaking as the voice of Captain Aesop on board the *Sarafand* boomed from the radio grille mounted above the view plates.

'This is the *Sarafand* speaking to all survey modules. Do not continue your approach. Cut your motors and remain where you are until further notification. This is an order.'

Before Aesop's voice had died away the radio silence that had been observed during the homeward race was broken as startled and angry comments from the other modules crashed from the loudspeaker. Surgenor felt the first cool feather-flick of alarm — Aesop had sounded as though something was seriously wrong. And *Module Five* was still churning its way down into the blackness of the polar plain.

'It must be some kind of fault in the mapping procedures,' Surgenor said, 'but you'd better cut the motors anyway.'

'But this is crazy! Aesop must be out of his tiny little mind. What could go wrong?' Voysey sounded indignant. He made no move to touch the motor controls.

Without warning an ultralaser burst from the *Sarafand* splintered the night into dazzling fragments and the hillside lifted skywards in front of *Module Five*. Voysey hit the brakes and the vehicle slid to a halt on the glowing edges of the ultralaser scar. Falling rock hammered on the roof in an irregular, deafening frenzy, then there was silence.

'I told you Aesop was out of his mind,' Voysey said numbly, almost to himself. 'Why did he do a thing like that?'

'This is the *Sarafand*,' the radio blared again. 'I repeat – no survey module is to attempt to approach the ship. I will be forced to destroy any other module which fails to obey this order.'

Surgenor pressed the button which put him in contact with the mother ship.

'This is Surgenor in *Module Five*, Aesop,' he said quickly. 'You had better tell us what's going on.'

'I intend to keep all crew members fully informed.' There was a pause, then Aesop spoke again. 'The problem is that six vehicles went out on this survey – and seven have come back. I hardly need to point out that this is one too many.'

*

With a spasm of alarm Candar realized he had made a mistake. His fear stemmed not from the fact that the strangers had discovered his presence among them, nor that they had reasonably potent weapons – it came from the knowledge that he had made such an elementary and avoidable error. The slow process of his physical and mental deterioration must have gone much further than he had appreciated.

The task of reforming his body to look like one of the travelling machines had been a difficult one, but not as difficult as the vast cellular reorganization which enabled him to survive when the two suns had grown huge and both were in the sky at once. His mistake had been in allowing the machine whose shape he had reproduced to come within range of the scanning device inside the large machine towards which the others were heading. He had allowed the small machine to draw away from him while he went through the agony of transformations and then, when he went after it, had become aware of the pulsing spray of electrons sweeping over him.

Crazed with hunger though he was, Candar had tested the fine sleet of particles and it occurred to him almost at once that they were being emitted by a surveillance system. He should have deduced in advance that creatures with the feeble sense organs he had perceived would have striven for something to widen their awareness of the universe – especially the creatures who would take the trouble to build such complicated vehicles. For an instant he considered absorbing all electrons which touched his skin, thereby rendering himself invisible to the scanning device, but decided that doing so would defeat his purpose. He was already within visual range of the largest machine, and the displaying of any unusual characteristics would make him instantly identifiable to the watchers inside.

Candar's alarm faded away as, with another part of his sensory network, he picked up the currents of fear and bewilderment stirring in the minds of the beings in the machine nearest to him. Minds like these, especially housed in bodies like these, could never present any serious problem – all he had to do was await the opportunity which was bound to occur very soon.

He crouched on the cracked surface of the plain, most of the metallic elements in his system transferred to the periphery of his new shape, which was now identical to that of the travelling machines. A small part of his energy was going into producing light, which he beamed out in front, and another minute fraction of it was

12

devoted to controlling the radiations reflected by his skin, thus obscuring his individuality.

He was Candar, the most intelligent, talented and powerful single entity in the universe – and all he had to do was wait.

The standard intercom speakers fitted in geodesic survey vehicles were, in spite of their small size, very effective pieces of equipment. Surgenor had never heard of one being overloaded before, but immediately following Aesop's announcement communication was lost as every module crew reacted in surprise or disbelief. A defence mechanism caused him to stare at the speaker grille in mild wonderment while another part of his mind assimilated Aesop's news.

A seventh module had appeared on an airless world which was not only uninhabited but, in the strictest clinical sense of the word, sterile. Not even the toughest known bacteria or virus could survive when Prila I ran the gamut of its double sun. It was totally unthinkable that an extra survey vehicle could have been awaiting the *Sarafand*'s arrival, and yet that was what Aesop claimed – and Aesop never made a mistake. The cacophony from the loudspeaker quieted abruptly as Aesop came on the air again.

'I am open for suggestions regarding our next move, but they must be made one at a time.'

The hint of reproof in Aesop's voice was enough to damp the noise level to a background rumble, but Surgenor could sense a growing panic. The root cause of the trouble was that operating a geodesic survey module had never become a genuine profession – because it was too easy. It was a casual, big-money job that smart young men went into for two or three years in order to raise capital for business ventures, and when signing on they practically demanded a written guarantee that there would never be any interruption in the profitable routine. Now, on this unprecedented occasion, something had gone wrong, and they were worried. Their jobs had been created largely by trade union pressures – it would have been a simple matter to automate the survey modules to the same extent as the mother ship – but at the first demand for a flexible response to an unforeseen event, the basis of the unions' arguments, they were both resentful and afraid.

Surgenor felt a flicker of annoyance at his team-mates, then remembered that he, too, was planning to pocket his profits and bow out. He had joined up sixteen years earlier, along with two of his space-struck cousins, and they had stayed for seven years before quitting and going into the plant-hire business. Most of his accumulated salary was in the business with them, but now Carl and Chris had reached the end of their patience and had presented him with an ultimatum. He had to take an active part in the running of the firm or be bought out, which was why he had served notice of resignation from the Cartographical Service. At the age of thirty-six he was going to settle down to a normal life, do a little desk-flying alleviated by some fishing and theatre-going, and probably find himself a reasonably compatible woman. Surgenor had to admit the prospect was not unpleasant. It was a pity that *Module Seven* had to crop up on his last trip.

'If there is a seventh module, Aesop—' Al Gillespie in *Three* spoke quickly '—another survey ship must have been here before us. Perhaps an emergency landing.'

'No,' Aesop replied. 'The local radiation levels rule that possibility right out. Besides, this is the only scheduled team within three hundred light-years.'

Surgenor pressed his talk button. 'I know this is just an offshoot of Al's suggestion, but have you checked for some kind of underground installation?'

'The world map is not yet complete, but I have run a thorough check on all the geonostic data. Result negative.'

Gillespie in *Three* spoke again. 'I take it that this new so-called module hasn't tried to communicate with the *Sarafand* or with any of the field crews. Why is that?'

'I can only surmise it is deliberately mingling with the others in order to get near the ship. At this stage I can't say why, but I don't like it.'

'What are we going to do?' The question was asked simultaneously and in varied forms by a number of men.

There was a lengthy silence before Aesop spoke. 'I ordered all modules to halt because I do not want to risk losing the ship, but my updated reading of the situation is that a certain amount of risk must be taken. I can only see three modules, and because the search pattern was broken over the last five hundred kilometres I cannot identify any of you by compass bearing alone. At least, not with a sufficiently high probability of being correct.

'I will therefore permit all modules – all seven of you – to approach the ship for visual inspection. The minimum separation that I will tolerate between the ship and any module is one thousand metres. Any module attempting to come closer – even by a single metre – will be destroyed. No warnings will be issued, so remember – one thousand metres.

'Commence your approach now.'

two

Surgenor, as the more experienced man, had considered taking control of *Module Five* as it drew nearer to the *Sarafand*, the pyramidical tower of lights which represented home and safety, but which now was a new and deadly source of danger. He knew that Aesop, having laid down the rules, would not hesitate for a fraction of a second to burn any vehicle which strayed across the invisible deadline. Voysey's earlier rashness appeared to have left him, however, and he made the approach in a circumspect manner which Surgenor could not fault. When the red-glowing digits on the range-finder showed that they still had fifty metres to go Voysey braked and shut down the drive. A silence descended over the cockpit.

'Close enough?' Voysey said. 'Or do you think we should edge up a bit further?'

Surgenor made a dampening movement with his hands. 'This is fine – it's best to allow for a margin of error in our ranging equipment and Aesop's.'

He scanned the forward screens and found that the only indication of other vehicles in the area was one distantly wavering light on the plain behind the big ship. Watching its glimmering progress, Surgenor speculated on whether the spark of light could be – he hesitated, then applied the label – the enemy.

'I wonder is that it,' Voysey said, echoing his own thoughts.

'Who knows?' Surgenor replied. 'Why don't you ask it?'

Voysey sat motionless for several seconds. 'All right. I will.' He pressed his talk button. 'This is *Module Five*, Voysey speaking. We are already at the ship. Who is the second module now approaching?'

'This is *Module One*, Lamereux speaking,' came a hearteningly familiar voice. 'Hello there, Victor, Dave. Good to see you – that's if it is you.'

'Of course it's us. Who else could it be?'

Lamereux's laugh sounded slightly unnatural. 'At a time like this I wouldn't even like to guess.'

Voysey released his talk button and turned to Surgenor. 'At least Aesop ought to be sure of us two now. I hope he spots a difference in the extra module and blows it away without any more talk. Before it makes a move.'

'What if it doesn't make a move?' Surgenor unwrapped a flavoured protein block and bit into it. He had planned that his next meal would be a triumphal banquet on board the mother ship, but now it looked as though dinner might be a little late.

'What do you mean about not making a move?'

'Well, even on Earth there are birds that imitate men's voices, monkeys that mimic their actions – and they haven't any special reason for doing it. That's just the way they are. This thing might be a super-mimic. A compulsive copier. Maybe it just turns into the same shape as any new thing it sees without even wanting to.'

'An animal that can mimic something the size of a survey module?' Voysey considered the idea for a moment, obviously not impressed. 'But why would it want to mingle with us?'

Behavioural mimicry. It saw us all converging on the *Sarafand* and was impelled to join us.

'I think you're gassing me again, Dave. I swallowed what you told us about those other freaks – Drambons, was it – but this is too much.'

Surgenor shrugged and ate more protein cake. He had seen the Drambons on his 124th planetary survey, wheel-shaped creatures on a high-gravity world who were the opposite of humans and indeed most other beings in that their blood remained stationary at the bottom of the wheel while their bodies circulated. He always had trouble convincing new survey men that Drambons really existed – Drambons and a hundred other equally bizarre species. That was the trouble with beta-space transportation, the

16

popularly named Instant Distant drive – it was the first form of travel which did not broaden the mind. Voysey was five thousand light-years from Earth, but because he had not done it the hard way, hopping from star to lonely star, he was mentally still inside the orbit of Mars.

Other lights began to flicker on *Module Five*'s viewscreens as the remaining vehicles made their appearances from behind hills or over folds in the terrain. They drew closer until there were seven ranged in a circle around the dimly etched black pinnacle of the *Sarafand*. Surgenor watched their progress with interest, hoping with part of his mind that the intruder would make the mistake of venturing across the invisible thousand-metre line.

Captain Aesop remained silent during the approach manoeuvres, but comment from the various crews crashed continuously from the radio grille. Some of the men, finding themselves still alive and unharmed as minute after minute went by, began to relax and make jokes about the situation. The banter died away as Aesop finally spoke from the lofty security of the ship's operations level, sixty metres above the surface of the plain.

'Before we listen to individual reports and such suggestions as may be available,' he said in an even voice, 'I wish to remind all crews of my instruction not to come nearer the ship than one thousand metres. Any module doing so will be destroyed without further warning.

'You may now,' Aesop concluded imperturbably, 'proceed with the discussion.'

Voysey snorted with resentment. 'Tea and cucumber sandwiches will be served presently! When I get back on board I'm going to take an axle wrench to Aesop and smash his . . . You'd think to hear him this is just some kind of kid's puzzle.'

'That's the way Aesop looks at everything.' Surgenor said. 'In this case, it's not a bad thing.'

The confident, reedy voice of Pollen in *Module Four* was the first to break the radio silence which had followed the announcement from the ship. This was Pollen's eighth survey and he was writing a book about his experiences, but had never allowed Surgenor to hear any of his recorded notes or see the written portion of the manuscript. Surgenor suspected it was because he, Surgenor, was portrayed in it as a risible Oldest Member figure.

'The way I see it,' Pollen began, 'the problem we have here takes the form of a classical exercise in logic.'

'It must be catching – he's talking the same way,' Voysey said, brooding.

'Turn it off Pollen,' somebody shouted angrily.

'All right, all right. But the fact remains that we can think our way out of this one. The basic parameters of the problem are these – we have six unmarked and identical survey modules and, hidden among them, a seventh machine . . .'

Surgenor pressed his talk button as an idea which had been forming in his mind suddenly coalesced. 'Correction,' he said quietly.

'Was that Dave Surgenor?' Pollen sounded impatient. 'As I was saying – we've only got to be logical. There is a seventh machine and it . . .'

'Correction.'

'That *is* Mr Surgenor, isn't it? What do you want Dave?'

'I want to help you be logical, Clifford. There isn't a seventh machine – we've got six machines and a very special kind of animal.'

'An animal?'

'Yes. It's a Grey Man.'

For the second time in an hour, Surgenor heard his radio loudspeaker fail to cope with the demands made on it, and he waited impassively for the noise to subside. He glanced sideways at Voysey's exasperated face and wondered if he, too, had looked like that the first time he had heard about Grey Men.

The stories were thinly spread, difficult to isolate from the Manichean fantasies which abounded in many cultures, but they cropped up here and there, on worlds where the native racial memory reached far enough into the past. There were distortions upon distortions, but always the same recognizable theme – that of the Grey Men and the great battle they had waged with and lost to the White Ones. Neither race had left any tangible traces of its existence to be picked up by Earth's belated armies of archaeologists, but the myths were there just the same.

And the most significant thing, to one whose intellectual ears were in tune, was that – no matter what the shape of the storytellers, or whether they walked, swam, flew, crawled or burrowed

18

– the name they applied to the Grey Men was always their own name for members of their own species. The noun was often accompanied by a qualifier which suggested anonymity, neutrality or formlessness ...

'What in hell is a Grey Man?' It was Carlen in *Module Three*.

'It's a big grey monster that can turn itself into anything it wants to,' Pollen explained. 'Mr Surgenor has one for a pet and he never travels anywhere without it – that's what started all those old stories.'

'It can't turn itself into anything it wants,' Surgenor said. 'It can only assume any external shape it wants. Inside it's still a Grey Man.'

There was another roar of disbelief intermingled with laughter.

'Getting back to this notion of yours about being logical,' Surgenor continued with deliberate stolidity, anxious to get the debate back on to a serious footing, 'why don't you at least *think* about what I'm saying and check it out. You don't have to accept my word.'

'I know, Dave – the Grey Man will vouch for everything you say.'

'What I'm proposing is that we ask Captain Aesop to go through the xenological data stores and estimate the probability of the existence of the Grey Men in the first place, and also the probability that *Module Seven* is a Grey Man.' Surgenor noted that this time there was no laughter and he was relieved because, if he was right, there was no time for irrelevancies. In fact, there was probably no time at all, for anything.

The bright double star, which was the world's parent sun, was hanging low in the sky beyond the dim bulk of the *Sarafand* and the distant black hills. In another seventeen months the planet would be threading its way between two points of light, and Surgenor wanted to be far away when that happened – but so did the multi-talented superbeast hidden in their midst.

Candar was astonished to find himself listening to the food creatures' mental processes with something approaching interest.

His race had never been machine-builders – they had relied instead on the strength, speed and adaptability of their great grey bodies. In addition to his instinctive disregard for machinery, Candar had spent seventy centuries on a world where no artifact, no matter how well-constructed, could survive the annual passage through the binary hell. Consequently he was shocked to realize how much the food creatures depended upon their fabrications of metal and plastics. The discovery which most intrigued him was that the metal shells were not only a means of transport, but that they actually supported the lives of the food creatures while they were on this airless world.

Candar tried to imagine entrusting his life to the care of a complicated and fallible mechanism, but the idea filled him with a cool, unfamiliar dread. He pushed it aside and concentrated all his ferocious intelligence on the problem of getting close enough to the spaceship to paralyse the nerve centres of the creatures within. In particular, it was necessary to immobilize the one they called Captain Aesop before the ship's weapons could be brought into play.

Gently, delicately, controlling his hunger, Candar prepared the attack.

Surgenor stared at his hand in disbelief.

He had decided to drink some coffee to ease the dryness in his throat and had begun to reach for the supply tube. His right hand had risen only a few millimetres, and then had dropped back on the armrest.

Surgenor's instinctive reaction was to bring his left hand over to assist the other, but it, too, refused to move – and the realization came that he was paralysed.

The mindless period of panic lasted perhaps a full minute, at the end of which Surgenor found himself exhausted from the conflict with his locked muscles. Serpents of icy sweat were making savage downward rushes over every part of his body. He forced himself to relax and assess the situation, discovering as he did so that he still had control of his eye movements.

A sideways glance showed him that Voysey had been caught, too – the only sign of life being a barely perceptible tremor of the facial muscles. Surgenor guessed the phenomenom was new to Voysey. It was the first time Surgenor had ever experienced it at first hand, but he had been on many worlds where animals of prey were able to surround themselves with a blanket field capable of suppressing the grosser neural activities in other creatures. The deadly talent was most often encountered on high gravity planets whose predators were likely to be as sluggish as their victims. Surgenor tried to speak to Voysey but, as he had expected, was unable to direct air through his vocal cords.

He suddenly became aware that voices were still issuing from the communications speaker, and had listened to them for a while before the full significance of the fact dawned on him.

'There isn't much to worry about,' Pollen was saying. 'This is the sort of exercise in pure logic which is right up your street, Aesop. I would suggest that you lead off by calling out the module numbers in rotation and commanding each to move back a hundred metres. Fifty metres would do, or even five – the distance doesn't really matter. The point is that by doing this you will separate the original six machines from the seventh, or on one of the commands *two* of the machines will . . .'

Surgenor swore mentally at his inability to reach his talk button and cut Pollen off before it was too late. He was desperately renewing his efforts to move one hand when, without warning, Pollen's voice was lost in a shrill discordant whistle of interference. The noise continued with no sign of abating and Surgenor knew, with a pang of relief, that *Module Seven* had stepped in to take control of the situation. Surgenor drove the tensions out of his muscles, concentrated on breathing steadily and evenly, and regained most of his ability to think. Pollen had been loudly and confidently signing their death warrants by making the mistake – in this case a fatal one – of confusing a theoretical proposition with the inimical realities of their predicament.

The situation on the black airless plain which glimmered in the viewscreens bore a superficial resemblance to the puzzles sometimes given in aptitude tests, and when treating it on that level Surgenor could see several solutions. Apart from Pollen's standard juggling-with-numbers technique, a more empirical approach would be to have Aesop fire a low-powered burst from a laser rifle at each module in turn. Even if a Grey Man were able to withstand that sort of treatment without flinching, spectroscope analysis of the light produced would almost certainly show up compositional differences. Another solution would be to order each module to unship the little inspection-and-repair robot which was used when conditions were too severe for manual work in protective suits. Surgenor doubted if the alien could cope with a simulation task which involved splitting itself into two independent sections.

21

The deadly flaw in all those solutions was that they employed a process of *elimination* – which was something *Module Seven* would never permit. Any attempt to narrow down the field would only have the effect of triggering off the final calamity a little earlier. The real-life solution, if one existed, must be capable of instantaneous application. And Surgenor was not at all optimistic about his chances of finding it.

From sheer force of habit he began reviewing the situation, searching for some lever which might be used to advantage, then he recalled the significance of the voices which had continued to issue from the communications speaker after he and Voysey had been struck dumb. Pollen and a number of the other crewmen were still able to talk, which probably meant they were out of *Module Seven*'s radius of control.

The discovery showed that the enemy had some limitations to its frightening power, but appeared to have no practical value. Surgenor examined the module's viewscreens, wondering just how many minutes or seconds were left. It was difficult to assimilate the discrete images properly without moving his head, but he saw that there were two other modules not far away to the right, which meant his own vehicle was part of a loose group of three. All the others were much farther away on the opposite side of the circle, and as he watched one of them began flashing its main light in a hesitant attempt at Morse.

Surgenor ignored it, partly because he had long forgotten the code and partly because he was concentrating his attention on the two nearer machines, one of which was almost certain to be *Module Seven*. High up on the *Sarafand* lights flickered against the background of stars as Aesop responded in crisp, high-speed Morse to the vehicle which had been attempting to communicate with him. Surgenor could imagine the consternation in that vehicle as its occupants tried to cope with Aesop's overtly efficient signalling.

The continuing screech of radio interference conspired with the sense of urgency to create a yammering in Surgenor's nerves and brain, rendering it almost impossible for him to bring his thoughts together. He understood the fallacy in trying to interpret alien behaviour patterns in terms of human attitudes – and a Grey Man had to be the most alien creature mankind was ever likely to encounter –

22

but there seemed to be something inconsistent about . . .

Voysey moved his right hand forward to the control console and activated the engines.

For an instant Surgenor thought they had been freed from the paralysis field, but he found himself still unable to move. Voysey's face was chalk-white and immobile, saliva glistening on his chin, and Surgenor realized he had acted merely as a human servo-mechanism, controlled by *Module Seven*. Surgenor's mind began to race.

This must be it, he thought, *our time is up.*

The only reason the alien could have for making Voysey activate the motors was that it was planning to move the vehicle to distract Aesop. Surgenor went cold at the idea – there was no way to distract or confuse Aesop, and he would not hesitate to vaporize the first module to cross the invisible thousand-metre line.

Voysey's left hand released the brakes and the vehicle shifted slightly on the uneven ground.

Surgenor made another frantic, despairing effort to move, but all that happened was that his panic returned in full force. What was *Module Seven*'s plan intended to achieve? He had deducted that its radius of control was limited. He also knew that it was about to trigger off an accident in the hope of drawing Aesop's attention away from itself, which almost certainly implied it was going to try getting closer to the *Sarafand*. But why? There was no point in such an action, unless . . .

His belated but full understanding of the situation expanded like a nova in Surgenor's mind – then new vistas of danger unfolded.

I know the truth, he thought, *but I mustn't think about it because a Grey Man is telepathic, and if he gets to know what I'm thinking . . .*

Vosey's hand thrust hard against the throttle levers and the module dipped forward.

. . . the Grey Man will learn that . . . NO! Think about anything else in the universe. Think about the past, the distant past, going to school, history lessons, history of science . . . the quantum nature of gravity was finally established in 2063, and the successful detection of the graviton led directly to an understanding of beta-space and thus to the development of faster-than-light travel . . . but nobody really understands what beta-space is like . . . no human being, that is . . . only . . . I almost did it . . . I almost thought about . . . I can't help it . . . AESOP!

*

The distance separating Candar from the spaceship was one that, in a more efficient form, he could have crossed in two bounds. It would take slightly longer this way, but he knew he was too fast to be stopped by anything. He gave full rein to his hunger, letting it drive him on as he leaped forward. Behind him, rather more slowly than he had expected, the two machines he had taken into his control rolled towards the spaceship. One of the food creatures was vainly trying to suppress a thought, but there was no time to study its meaning ...

Changing shape as he went, Candar got safely within control distance. Exulting, he struck with his brain, hurling the intangible nets of mind-force which induced paralysis in lesser creatures.

Nothing!

An ultralaser beam hit him with a violence which would have annihilated any other being within microseconds, but Candar could not die so easily. The pain was greater than he could ever have expected, but even worse than the agony was his sudden clear understanding of the minds of the food creatures – those bleak, cold, alien minds.

For the first time ever, Candar felt fear.

Then he died.

The champagne was good, the steak was good, and sleep – when it finally came – would be even better.

Surgenor leaned back contentedly, lit his pipe, and gazed benignly at the eleven other men seated at the long table in the *Sarafand*'s mess room. During the meal he had reached a decision, and he knew with a comforting glow in his belly that, for him, it was the right decision. He had made up his mind that he *liked* being an Oldest Member figure. Shrewd young men could go on putting him in their books of space travel reminiscences, his cousins could buy him out of their plant-business – he was going to stay with the Cartographical Service until he had satiated mind and soul with the sight of new worlds. It was his life, his way of life, and he had no intention of giving it up.

At the other end of the table, Clifford Pollen was making his notes of the trip.

'The way you see it Dave,' Pollen said, 'is that the Grey Man was simply incapable of understanding the machine-building phil-osophy?'

'That's right. A Grey Man, because of his special physical properties, would have no use for a machine at the best of times. And thousands of years on a planet like Prila I – where a machine couldn't exist anyway – would have conditioned his mind to the point where our machine-orientated lives would have been incom-prehensible to him.'

Surgenor drew on the fragrant smoke, and he felt an unexpected surge of sympathy for the massive alien being whose remains still lay on the black rock of the planet they had left behind. Life would have been very precious to a Grey Man, too precious for him ever to consider entrusting it to anyone or anything but himself. That, basically, was why he had made the mistake of trying to control the entity which the *Sarafand*'s crew thought of as Captain Aesop.

Wondering how the Grey Man felt in that final moment of dis-covery, Surgenor glanced at the discreet identification plate on the nearest of the terminals belonging to the ship's central computer installation – that vast artificial intelligence into whose keeping they delivered their lives at the beginning of each survey. The plate said:

A.E.S.O.P.

Surgenor had heard the crewmen guess that the letters stood for Advanced Electronic Spaceship Operator and Pilot – but nobody was absolutely sure. Human beings, he suddenly realized, tend to take a lot for granted.

three

Space had different ways of punishing those who ventured into it. The physical danger was always present, like a threat that was whispered over and over again, and yet it was not the quality of the environment which weighed most heavily on the travellers' minds. Space was hostile to human life, but it was more forgiving of errors than some other media – for example, the depths of an ocean – in which men had learned to live and work with almost complete equanimity. Its most potent weapon was, simply, its size.

No size of standing on hilltops on dark nights and surveying the heavens could prepare a man for the actuality of space travel, because the earthbound observer saw only the stars, not what separated them. They glittered in his vision, filling his eyes, and he had no choice but to assign them to a position of importance in the cosmic scheme. The space traveller saw things differently. He was made aware that the universe consisted of *emptiness*, that suns and nebulae were almost an irrelevancy, that the stars were nothing more than a whiff of gas diffusing into infinity. And sooner or later that knowledge began to hurt.

There were no abrupt descents into psychosis among the Cartographical Service crews – the preliminary screening saw to that – and indeed it was rare for the men who drove the survey modules to philosophize about the meaning of their existence, but the stresses imposed by their way of life took a toll just the same. Loneliness and homesickness were occupational diseases. Only uninhabited worlds were surveyed by the Service, quickly sating the mapping crews with views of desert, barren rock and tundra to the point at which they began to pray for something unforeseen to occur, even if it involved hardship or extra danger. But incidents were so rare that a simple mechanical failure would provide conversational fodder for many months.

Against that background, men tended to complete the two years demanded by their employment contracts, follow up with one extra tour which proved to themselves and their friends that they could have gone on indefinitely, and then take their gratuities and retreat to occupations which would enable them to remain at home.

A few men, like Dave Surgenor, had the capacity to endure in the Service regardless of the intellectual and emotional hazards. The *Sarafand*, therefore, was akin to most other ships in having a cadre of veterans whose lot it was to partner less experienced men in the modules and oversee their progress. They also performed a valuable service, though one for which there was no official recognition, in that they created a stable group identity to which newcomers could relate. Surgenor had seen scores of men – and an occasional woman – come and go, and over the years had developed a wry, avuncular approach to their adjustment problems. Although he sometimes grumbled about the brashness of novices, he had to admit that they helped relieve the monotony of shipboard life.

A year had passed since the encounter with the Grey Man on Prila I, a year of completely routine survey work, and in that time two crew changes had occurred. One man had left the Service, another had transferred to a more modern ship of the Mark Eight class, and both had been replaced by recent recruits. Surgenor had watched the newcomers with unobtrusive interest and had formed the opinion that the more likeable of the pair was, unfortunately, the less likely to remain long in the Service. Bernie Hilliard was a talkative youngster who appeared to enjoy sparking his ideas against the flint of Surgenor's well-established attitudes. And the breakfast hour, when he was fresh from sleep, was his favourite time for conversational fencing.

'What you don't appreciate, Dave,' he said one morning, 'is that I was *home* last night. With my wife. I was *there*.'

Hilliard leaned across the breakfast table as he spoke, pink face childishly solemn with conviction, his blue eyes imploring Surgenor to accept what he was saying, to share the joy which was so freely offered. Surgenor felt well-rested and well-fed, and therefore was in a mood to agree with almost anything – but there were problems. His mind fastened obstinately on the knowledge that the *Sarafand* was making its way through a dense star cluster many thousands of light-years from Hilliard's home in Saskatchewan. There was also the obtrusive fact that young Hilliard was not married.

Surgenor shook his head. 'You dreamed you were home.'

'You still don't get it!' Exasperation and evangelist zeal caused Hilliard, who was normally quiet in his manner, to bounce on his chair. Men at the other end of the long table glanced curiously in his direction. The ship-day had just begun and the lighting panels in the semi-circular room, typical of spacecraft living quarters, were glowing most strongly at the end designated 'east'.

'The experience of using a Trance-Port has little resemblance to ordinary dreaming,' Hilliard continued. 'A dream is only a dream, and when you're awake you recognize the memories of it as being nothing but dream memories. But with a Trance-Port tape you are *transported*, in the old sense of the word – that's the reason for their name – into another existence. The recollections you have next day are indistinguishable from other memories. I tell you, Dave, they are completely real.'

Surgenor poured himself a fresh cup of coffee. 'But right now, this morning, you know you weren't in Canada a few hours ago. And you do know that you were bunked down in this ship on the deck above this room. Alone.'

'Pinky was alone, all right,' Tod Barrow – the second of the new men – put in, winking at the others. 'I tried to slip into his room last night for a good-night kiss, but the door was locked. At least, I hope he was alone.'

'Incompatability doesn't make a memory any less real,' Hilliard said, ignoring the interruption. 'What about all those times you were sure you had done something like packing a toothbrush, and then found you hadn't? Even when it's been proved that you didn't pack the toothbrush you still go on "remembering" how you did it. Same thing.'

'Is it?'

'Of course it is.'

'It all sounds a bit strange to me,' Surgenor said doubtfully, taking refuge in his Oldest Member role, a part which was becoming progressively easier to play with each new voyage he made for the Cartographical Service. The mapping crews seemed to get younger every year and to demand a degree of pampering which would have been unheard of when he had first signed on.

In earlier days it had been accepted that there would be occasional periods of inactivity and boredom. These usually occurred during normal-space planetary approaches or when the ship got into a region which was so congested that the instantaneous drive could not be used to its full extent. The traditional therapy – mainly consisting of poker sessions and increased liquor rations – was one which Surgenor appreciated and understood, and he had visited the recent experimental introduction of Trance-Port tapes without enthusiasm.

'The most important thing about the tapes,' Hilliard went on, 'is that they ease the pressure of loneliness. The human nervous system can only stand this sort of life for a strictly limited period, and then something has to give.'

'That's why I tried to get into Pinky's room last night,' Barrow said, grinning evilly. He was a former computer engineer and an abrasive individual who made a profession out of being dark, hairy and masculine. From his first hour on the ship he had been verbally

28

sniping at Hilliard over the latter's baby-pink face and fuzz of blond hair.

'Shamble off and discover fire or invent the wheel or something,' Hilliard said to him casually, without turning his head. 'I'm telling you, Dave, you can only take it for so long.'

Surgenor waved a confident denial with his cup. 'I've been in the Service for seventeen years – without any dream tapes to stop me going crazy.'

'Oh! Sorry, Dave – I wasn't implying anything. Honest.'

The profuseness of the apology and the gleam in the youngster's eyes aroused Surgenor's suspicions. 'Are you trying to be funny, junior? Because if you are ...'

'Relax, Dave,' Victor Voysey said from two places along the table. 'We all know you're incurably sane. Bernie just wants you to try a tape for a while to see what it's like. I'm using one myself this trip – got me a nice little Chinese firecracker of a wife I go home to most evenings. It's a good life, Dave.'

Surgenor stared at him in surprise. Voysey was a red-haired freckle-skinned man with serious blue eyes and a pragmatic outlook on life which was helping him develop into an excellent surveyer. He had been sharing *Module Five* with Surgenor for more than a year, and looked like building up a respectable record of service. This was the first time he had mentioned going on to the tapes.

'You do it? You put one of those metal pie dishes under your pillow when you bunk down at night?' Surgenor spoke with a kind of amiable scorn he knew would not hurt the other man's feelings too much.

'Not every night.' Voysey looked slightly uncomfortable as he picked at his ham and eggs.

Surgenor felt his puzzlement increase. 'You didn't tell me.'

'Well, it isn't the sort of thing you go around talking about.' An incongruous tinge of crimson appeared in Voysey's cheeks. 'The Trance-Port programmes give you a developing relationship with a nice girl, and it's sort of private. Just like in real life.'

'*Better* than in real life – you know you're going to score every time,' Barrow said, making piston movements with his fist. 'Tell us all about your Chinese piece, Vic. Is it like they say?'

'I wasn't talking to you.'

Barrow was unabashed. 'Come on, Vic – I'll tell you about my little woman. I only want to know if . . .'

'Shut it!' Voysey, his face losing its colour, picked up his fork and held it under Barrow's slate-grey chin. 'I don't want to talk to you, and I don't want you to talk to me, and the next time you butt in on me I promise I'll do some permanent damage.'

There was a taut silence, then Barrow got to his feet, muttering indignantly, and moved down the table to the other side of the small group. 'What's the matter with him?' he whispered to Surgenor. 'What did I say?'

Surgenor shook his head. He had no liking for Barrow, but Voysey's reaction had seemed unnecessarily violent. All Surgenor knew about the Trance-Ports was that they were triggered by the pressure of a man's head on the pillow, and worked largely by direct cortical stimulation of words and images. Initially they produced a mild form of hypnosis which promoted sleep, and then – after the brain rhythms had begun to indicate sleep, and when periods of rapid eye movement showed that the subject was ready to dream – fed his mind with a programmed scenario.

To Surgenor the Trance-Port players were little more than a type of advanced movie projector, and therefore he was puzzled by the depth of the feelings they seemed to engender. He leaned towards Voysey, who was now staring down at his plate, but Hilliard caught his arm.

'Victor's right in what he says about it being just like real life,' Hilliard said, with a warning frown which indicated that Voysey should be left alone. 'A Trance-Port isn't an erotic dream machine. The psychologists who programme the tapes realize you need something more than that when you're this far from home. A sexy girl is always the central figure, of course, but she's a lot of other things besides sexy. Warm. Understanding. Fun to be with, yet dependable. She provides you with all the things that Service life lacks.'

'And she doesn't cost you a cent,' Barrow said gleefully, apparently recovered from his brush with Voysey.

Hilliard was not put off. 'She becomes very important to a man, Dave. I guess that's why anybody who is Trance-Porting doesn't talk about it much.'

'You're talking some.'

'I am, aren't I?' Hilliard smiled like a schoolboy announcing his first date. He lowered his voice to exclude Barrow. 'It must be because I'm feeling so good. I never had an entirely satisfactory relationship with any of the girls I knew back in Saskatoon. There was always something missing.'

'Something missing?' Barrow said. 'In your case it's easy to guess what.' He glanced up and down the table, trying to enlist smiles, but he had made no friends since joining the *Sarafand* and the faces of the module crews remained impassive.

Hilliard, seizing the psychological moment, got to his feet and spoke in his best high-school declamatory style. 'Barrow,' he said solemnly, 'if you had as much ability to hurt people as you obviously have the desire, you'd be a deadly conversationalist indeed – as it is, you are merely pathetic.'

There was an admiring whoop of laughter along the table. Hilliard acknowledged it with a dignified nod and sat down again, seemingly oblivious to Barrow's look of hatred. Surgenor was pleased for the young man, but he had some misgivings about the developing situation, which was another symptom of the strain felt by the *Sarafand*'s personnel.

The trip had already lasted longer than expected when it was discovered that Martell's Cluster had four more planetary systems than had been indicated by long-range examination. It was within Aesop's discretion to reject the four extra surveys, but he had taken the decision to press on. Surgenor, filled with an uncharacteristic wish to reach Earth in time to spend Christmas with his cousins and their families, had voiced objections, only to have them dismissed. Now, with tension building up around the breakfast table, he decided to have yet another private interview with Aesop.

Hilliard, resuming where he left off, said, 'Things are different now that I've met Julie.'

'Julie? You mean, they have names?'

'Of course they have names!' Hilliard covered his face with his hands for a few seconds. 'You just don't understand, do you, Dave? Real girls have names, so Trance-Port girls have names. Mine happens to be called Julie Cornwallis.'

At that moment Surgenor became aware of two simultaneous events. A chime sounded and Aesop spoke to the crew on the general address system, telling them he had assessed all gravitational forces acting on the ship and was about to make a beta-space jump closer to the heart of Martell's Cluster. And, while the omni-directional voice of the computer was flooding the room, the face of Tod Barrow – which had been filled with broody resentment – suddenly registered surprise and happiness. The look was quickly gone, and in any case could have been interpreted as pleasure over Aesop's announcement.

The incident was less than trivial, and Surgenor forgot it as the module crews abandoned the table and crowded into the dimness of the observation room on the same deck. He went with them, moving with a casual stride which befitted a veteran of many such star jumps, yet contriving to be among the leaders. Watching the Instant Distance drive in action, seeing the star fields abruptly shift and knowing he had covered light-years with the speed of thought, was an experience Surgenor could never regard as commonplace.

The observation room had twelve swivel chairs – one for each member of the ship's company – which were grouped midway between two hemispherical viewing screens. Forward was a view through the centre of Martell's Cluster. The curved screen was like a bowl of black champagne, frozen, with a thousand silver bubbles checked in flight by the briefness of man's existence. Surgenor waited for the jump, trying to feel it happening, even though he knew that any process which was slow enough to be perceived would probably be fatal.

On the instant, with no sense of anything having moved, the disc of a new sun appeared, seemingly to have driven the other stars outwards.

'We've arrived,' Clifford Pollen said, acknowledging the fact that Aesop had taken them right into the target system, and looking furtively grateful for yet another safe transit. Pollen, still gathering material for his projected book, was a connoisseur of legends about ships which had essayed routine jumps, and in the beta-space universe – where the gravitation flux was like a storm howling among the galaxies – had been swept away by freak eddies, to emerge in normal-space at points remote from their destinations. Surgenor knew there were regions where the inter-galactic wind penetrated chinks in the gravity shield of the Milky Way, but their locations and boundaries had been well charted. He had no qualms about the Instant Distance Drive, and derived a gently malicious pleasure from Pollen's enduring nerviness.

The next few weeks would be occupied by normal-space approaches to planets and, where feasible, direct examination by the survey modules. Depending on how things went, the *Sarafand* could spend a full month in the present system, and there were three others yet to be visited.

Surgenor looked at the alien sun and thought about the precious fleeting afternoons of winter on Earth, about football matches and cigar stores and women at supper tables, and about the deep comforts of families drawing together at Christmas. And he knew that Aesop was wrong, that the voyage should not have been extended. He stood up without speaking and went to the island of privacy which was his room. Not bothering to lock the door – a rule of shipboard life was that no crewman ever entered another's quarters uninvited – he sat down and closed his eyes.

'Hear these words,' he said presently, using the code phrase which put any member of the ship's company on to the computer.

'I'm listening to you, David,' Aesop said mildly, voice accurately beamed to Surgenor's ears.

'It was a mistake to include four extra system surveys in this mission.'

'Is that an opinion? Or are you in possession of data which have not been made available to me?' A dryness had crept into Aesop's voice and Surgenor was almost certain that the choice of words constituted sarcasm, but he had never been able to establish the exact degree of verbal subtlety of which Aesop was capable.

'I'm giving you my assessment of the situation,' he said. 'There's a lot of tension building up in the crew.'

'That is predictable. I have made allowances for it.'

'You can't predict how human beings will react.'

'I did not say I could predict their actions,' Aesop said patiently. 'I can assure you, though, that I weighed every important factor before making my decision.'

'What factors?'

There was a barely perceptible pause, an indication that Aesop considered the question a stupid one, before the computer spoke. 'The volume of space explored by the Cartographical Service is roughly spherical. As the radius of this sphere increases, its surface area . . .'

'I know all that stuff,' Surgenor interrupted. 'I know the Bubble is growing and that the job gets bigger all the time and that there's an economic pressure to extend the missions. I was asking about the human factors. What do you go on when you're trying to assess them?'

'Apart from the body of general psychological data available to me, I can refer you to the relevant abstracts from Mission Final Reports for the past century. Those of the Cartographical Service alone occupy some eight million words; military records, more extensive because of the nature of the activities, run to fifteen million words; then there are the reports of the various civilian agencies which . . .'

'Forget it.' Surgenor, aware that he was being out-manoeuvred, decided to try a different approach. 'Aesop, I've been with you on the *Sarafand* a long time, long enough to start thinking of you as a human being, and I believe I can speak to you just as one man would talk to another.'

'Before you begin, David, will you answer two questions?'

'Of course.'

'One – what gave you the curious notion that I would be subject to flattery? Two – where did you get the even more curious idea that ascribing human attributes to me could possibly be construed as flattery?'

'I have no answers to those questions,' Surgenor said heavily, defeated.

'That is a pity. Proceed.'

'Proceed with what?'

'I'm ready for you to speak to me as one man would talk to another.'

Surgenor did exactly that for almost a minute.

'Now that you have relieved your mental stresses,' Aesop commented at the end of the outburst, 'please be reminded that the correct code phrase for verbal disengagement is "Hear me no more".'

Surgenor tried for a final obscenity as the audio connection was broken, but his imagination failed him. He prowled around the room for a while, forcing himself to accept the realization that there was no way of getting back to Earth by Christmas, then went down to the hangar deck and began carrying out system checks on his survey module. At first he found it difficult to concentrate, but then his professionalism took over and several hours went by quickly. The light panels at the 'noon' section of the circular deck were glowing brightest, giving the impression of a midday sun beyond, when he emerged from the vehicle and went to lunch. He sat down beside Hilliard.

'Where have you been?' Pollen said.

'Checking out my sensor banks.'

'Again?' Pollen raised one eyebrow in amusement, his slightly prominent teeth glistening.

'It keeps him out of mischief,' Hilliard said, winking at the others.

'I've never had to backtrack halfway round a planet,' Surgenor replied, reminding Pollen of an incident he was anxious to forget, and specified his meal on the menu buttons. His soup had just emerged from the dispensing turret when Tod Barrow came into the mess and, after surveying the table, sat down opposite him. Barrow, who had evidently been working out in the gymnasium, was wearing a track suit and smelled of fresh sweat. He greeted Surgenor with unexpected and excessive joviality.

Surgenor gave him a slow nod. 'Is the shower unit out of action?'

'How would I know?' Barrow looked innocently surprised at the question.

'People usually go there after a workout.'

'Hell, only dirty people need to keep washing themselves,' Barrow's slate-grey features creased in a grin as his eyes fixed on Hilliard. 'Besides, I was in the tub last night. At home. With my wife.'

'Not another one,' Surgenor muttered.

Barrow ignored him, keeping his gaze on Hilliard. 'Real fancy tub, it is. Gold. Just matches my wife's hair.'

Surgenor noticed that Hilliard, beside him, had set down his fork and was staring at Barrow with a peculiar intensity.

'Her skin's sort of gold-coloured, as well,' Barrow continued. 'And when we're in the tub together she ties her hair up with a gold ribbon.'

'What's her name?' Hilliard said, surprising Surgenor with the question.

35

'Even the faucets are gold on that tub. Gold dolphins.' Barrow's face was ecstatic. 'We shouldn't have really bought it, but when we saw it in . . .'

'*What's her name?*' Hilliard's chair tumbled behind him as he jumped to his feet.

'What's the matter with you, Pinky?'

'For the last time, Barrow – tell me her name.' Red beacons of anger burned in Hilliard's cheeks.

'It's Julie,' Barrow announced contentedly. 'Julie Cornwallis.'

Hilliard's jaw sagged. 'You're a liar.'

'I ask you,' Barrow said to the others who were watching the incident, 'is that any way to speak to a shipmate?'

Hilliard leaned across the table towards him. 'You're a bloody liar, Barrow.'

'Hey, Bernie!' Surgenor stood up and caught Hilliard's arm. 'Cool off a little.'

'You don't understand, Dave.' Hilliard shook his arm free. 'He's claiming he's got a Trance-Port tape the same as mine, but the supply office doesn't do that. They make sure there's only one of each type on a ship.'

'They must have made a mistake,' Barrow said, chuckling. 'Anybody can make a mistake.'

'Then you can turn yours in and get a different one.'

Barrow shook his head emphatically. 'No chance, Pinky. I'm happy with the one I got.'

'If you don't turn it in I'll . . .'

'Yes, Pinky?'

'I'll . . .'

'My soup is getting cold,' Surgenor said in his loudest voice. He was a big deep-chested man and could produce an awe-inspiring bellow when he thought it necessary. 'I'm not going to eat cold soup for anybody – so we're all going to sit here quietly and take our food like grown-ups.' He picked up Hilliard's chair and pushed the younger man into it.

'You don't understand, Dave,' Hilliard whispered. 'It's like my home has been invaded.'

For a reply, Surgenor pointed at his soup and began to spoon it up in silent concentration.

*

In the 'afternoon' Surgenor finished reading a book, spent some time in the observation room, then went to the gymnasium and practised fencing with Al Gillespie. He saw nothing of Hilliard or Barrow, and if he thought about the incident of the Trance-Port tapes at all it was only to congratulate himself on having forced some sense into the two men concerned. Peaceful red-gold light was flooding through the 'western' end of the mess when he entered and sat down. Most of the places were filled and the dispensing turret was busy whirring up and down the table's central slot.

The lively atmosphere would normally have made Surgenor feel cheerful, but on this occasion it served to remind him of Christmas he was not going to have on Earth, of the bleak new year that would begin in the absence of an afterglow from the old. He dropped into a chair, called up a standard dinner and was eating without much pleasure when he became aware of a latecomer sitting down beside him. His spirits sank even further when he saw it was Tod Barrow.

'Sorry I'm late, men,' Barrow said, 'but I see you've started without me.'

'We took a vote on it,' Sig Carlen growled, 'and decided that was what you would want us to do.'

'Quite right.' Barrow stretched luxuriously, immune to sarcasm. 'I was dozing most of the afternoon, so I decided to go home. To see my wife.'

There was a groan of complaint from the assembly.

'That Julie is some girl,' Barrow continued, heedless, closing his eyes the better to savour his memories. 'The way she dresses you'd think she was a Sunday school teacher or something – but what a line in undies.'

Somebody at the other end of the table gave an appreciative guffaw. Surgenor glanced around, looking for Hilliard, and saw him sitting with his head bowed. There was a rigid stillness about the young man which Surgenor did not like.

Surgenor leaned closer to Barrow, meeting his gaze squarely. 'Why don't you give it a rest?'

Barrow waved a dismissive hand. 'But you've got to *hear* this. Lotsa married women will only perform in bed, but my Julie has a habit of . . .' He stopped speaking and a grin spread over his face as Hilliard jumped to his feet and ran from the room. 'Aw, look at that! Young Pink's gone and left us, just as I was getting to the good bit.

37

Perhaps he's gone to warn Julie about two-timing him.' More laughter greeted the remark and Barrow looked gratified.

'You're laying it on too thick,' Surgenor told him. 'Leave the kid alone.'

'It's only a joke. He should be able to take a joke.'

'You should be able to make one.'

Barrow shrugged and, apparently having satisfied himself as regards getting even with Hilliard, scanned his menu display. He ordered corn-and-crab soup and took it slowly, pausing every now and then to shake his head and chuckle. Surgenor tried to repress the anger he felt at Barrow for being such a disruptive influence, at Hilliard for allowing himself to get so worked up over nothing more than a piece of dream tape, at the Service psychologists for issuing the Trance-Ports in the first place, and at Aesop for prolonging the trip beyond its normal term. The effort stretched his tolerance to the limit.

He was toying with the remains of his meat loaf when the conversational hum in the room faded away. Surgenor looked up and saw that Bernie Hilliard, unnaturally pale, had come back into the room. The young man walked around the table and came to a halt beside Barrow, who twisted in his chair to look up at him.

'What's on your mind, Pinky?' Barrow seemed slightly taken aback by the new development.

'That soup you're eating looks a bit thin,' Hilliard said woodenly. 'What do you think?'

Barrow looked puzzled. 'Seems all right to me.'

'No. It's definitely too thin – try some noodles.' Hilliard produced a tangle of silver-and-green tape from behind his back and slapped it down into the other man's soup.

'Hey! What is this?' Barrow stared at the knotted mass and suddenly was able to supply his own answer. 'That's a Trance-Port tape!'

'Correct.'

'But ...' Barrow's eyes shuttled as he reached an inevitable conclusion. 'It's *my* tape!'

'Right again.'

'That means you went into my room.' Barrow sent a scandalized glance around the other men, making them witnesses to the confession, then he leapt at Hilliard's throat. Hilliard tried to twist free and both men fell to the floor, with Barrow uppermost.

'You shouldn't ... have gone ... into my room!' Still holding Hilliard by the throat, Barrow punctuated his words by hammering the young man's head against the floor.

Surgenor, who had risen from his place, lifted one foot and stamped it down hard between Barrow's shoulder blades. Barrow collapsed like a pile of sticks and lay on his side, gasping, while Surgenor and Voysey picked Hilliard up.

'Do me a favour, Bernie, for God's sake,' Surgenor said. 'Try to unscramble your brains.'

'Sorry, Dave.' Hilliard looked shaken, but triumphant. 'He had no right ...'

'You had no right to go into his room – that's one thing you just don't do shipboard.'

'Yeah, how about that?' Barrow put in, struggling to his feet. 'He violated my privacy.'

'Not as much as you violated mine,' Hilliard said.

'It was *my* tape.' Barrow turned and lifted the dripping tangle from his plate. 'Anyway, a smear of soup won't do it any harm. I'll clean it and feed it back in the cassette.'

'Go ahead.' Hilliard paused to smile. 'But it won't do you any good – I wiped it first.'

Barrow swore and moved towards Hilliard again, but was pushed down into his chair by several men acting in concert. Surgenor was relieved to see that the general weight of opinion was against Barrow – a situation less likely to get out of hand than one where there were two evenly matched sides. Barrow surveyed the ring of unfriendly faces for a moment, then gave an incredulous laugh.

'Look at them! All screwed up over nothing! Relax, men, relax!' He dropped the green-and-silver tape back into his soup and pretended to spoon it into his mouth. 'Hey, this is good stuff, Pinky – I think you found the best thing to do with these stinking Trance-Ports.'

A number of men laughed, and there was an immediate easing of tension. Barrow clowned his way through the rest of the meal, giving an excellent impression of a man who was incapable of bearing a grudge. But Surgenor, watching him closely, was unable to accept that it was anything more than an impression. He left the table with a premonition that the episode was far from ended.

four

'Hear these words,' Surgenor said to the quietness of his room.

'I'm listening to you, Dave.'

'Things are getting worse.'

'That statement is too generalized to have any . . .'

'Aesop!' Surgenor took a deep breath, reminding himself there was no point in getting angry at a computer no matter how articulate the machine might be. 'I'm talking about the psychological stress on the survey crews. The signs of strain are becoming more pronounced.'

'I have observed pulse rates going up and skin resistance going down, but only on isolated occasions. There is no cause for alarm.'

'No cause for alarm, he says. Aesop, does it occur to you that I – because I'm a human being – could know more about what goes on inside human beings than you do? I mean, you can never really know what's going on inside a man's head.'

'I am more concerned with his actions, but should I need information concerning the mental states of crew members I can refer to the relevant abstracts from Mission Final Reports for the past century. Those of the Cartographical Service alone occupy some eight million words; military records, more extensive because of . . .'

'Don't go through all that again.' A new thought struck Surgenor. 'Supposing there was cause for alarm, suppose things really started getting out of control – what could you possibly do about it?'

Aesop's voice was peaceful. 'I could do many things, David, but the indications are that adding a simple psychotropic drug to the drinking water would be quite sufficient to restore a stable condition.'

'You're empowered to tranquillize human beings any time you feel like it?'

'No – only when they feel like it.'

Again, Surgenor was almost certain that the linguistic subtlety built into the computer was being used to mock him. 'Even that's too often for my liking. I wonder how many people know about this.'

'It is impossible to compute how many people know, but I can give a relevant piece of information.'

'Which is ...'

'That – no matter how many more you decide to tell – you will not be back on Earth by the twenty-fifth of December.'

Surgenor stared coldly at the speaker grille on the wall of his room. 'Read me like a book, did you?'

'Not really, David – I find books quite difficult to read.'

'Aesop, do you know you have a nasty supercilious streak?'

'The adjectives are inapplicable in my ...' Aesop broke off in mid-sentence – something Surgenor had never known him to do before. There was a pause, then the voice returned, more rapid now and charged with designed-in urgency. 'There is a fire on the hangar deck.'

'Serious?' Surgenor grabbed for his boots and began pulling them on.

'Moderate concentration of smoke, but I detect only a localized blaze and there are no electrical circuits registering. The situation appears to be well within the capacity of my automatic systems.'

'I'll go down and have a look,' Surgenor said, relaxing a little as the spectre of a major catastrophe receded. He left the room and ran to the main companionway, slid down it and sprinted to the head of the stair which led below. It was crowded with men who were anxious to find out what had happened. The circular hangar deck was hazed with oily drifting smoke which obscured the outlines of the six survey vehicles in their stalls, but even as Surgenor entered he could see that it was being efficiently drawn into the ceiling grilles. In little more than a minute the smoke had vanished except for stray whiffs arising from a box on one of the workbenches.

'I have turned off the fire-control sonics,' Aesop announced. 'Complete the extinction manually.'

'Look at this.' Voysey got to the workbench first and picked up a small laser knife which was lying with its projection head pointing at a smouldering box which contained oily waste. 'Somebody left this cutter switched on low power.' He studied the tool curiously. 'This thing's dangerous. The range limit is broken – that's what started the fire.'

While one of the men broke out a fire-control grenade and fumed it into the box, Surgenor took the cutter from Voysey and examined it. The range-control plate had been twisted completely out of line in a way which, to him, did not look accidental. Another odd fact was that the waste box with the charred hole in its side invariably sat on the floor with clamps securing it to the leg of the bench. It was almost as if somebody had started the fire deliberately, but that was something no sane person would do. A spaceship was a machine for keeping human beings alive against all the dictates of nature, and it was unthinkable that anybody should try to damage the machine . . .

'I guess we were lucky,' Voysey said. 'There's no harm done.'

Aesop spoke immediately. 'That remains to be seen, gentlemen. The hangar deck was in the clean air condition for electronics maintenance on *Modules One*, *Three* and *Six*. All exposed units will have to be inspected for contamination, then cleaned and given function checks. I suggest that you begin work on them now – otherwise there could be delays in the forthcoming survey.'

Groans of protest were heard from a number of men, but Surgenor fancied that most of them were pleased at having some genuinely necessary task to perform. It created a break in the shipboard routine and gave them a comforting sense of being useful. He joined in the work, putting aside his speculations about the origins of the fire, and spent two hours engrossed in checking out electronics packs. The survey modules were designed for repair by replacement to a large extent, so that relatively untrained men could keep them operational, but in spite of that the job of inspecting and changing major components was one which demanded concentration. As always, Aesop assisted in and monitored the various tasks. His long-range diagnostic microscopes, mounted on the ceiling, made sporadic movements as they projected enormously magnified pictures of circuits on to large screens.

By the time the evening meal was supplied by the auto-kitchen Surgenor was deeply but pleasantly tired. He was relieved, therefore, when the meal passed off without any more trouble between Hilliard and Barrow. After they had eaten, most of the complement watched a holoplay. Surgenor had two large whiskies, found himself growing dangerously nostalgic about Earth at Christmas, and went to bed early.

He awoke in the morning, relaxed, filled with the knowledge that it was Saturday and that he would not be going to his office. The design he was producing for the new university auditorium was at a fascinating, mind-devouring stage, but he knew from experience that a weekend of complete rest would enable him to return to the project at an even higher pitch of enthusiasm and efficiency. Contentment filled his mind like the chiming of silver bells as he turned in his bed and reached for Julie.

There was a momentary disappointment as he discovered her place was empty, then he became aware of the aroma of brewing coffee drifting upstairs from the kitchen. He got up, stretched, and padded naked into the bathroom and stood for a moment looking at the tub with its taps in the shape of gold dolphins. He decided against having a bath and turned on the shower in the adjoining smoked-glass unit. Cherry blossoms gleamed like sunlit snow beyond the bathroom windows, and in the distance an enthusiastic gardener was busy with a lawn mower, performing the first rites of spring.

'Dave?' Julie's voice was faint above the sound of the water. 'Are you up? Want some coffee?'

'Not yet.' Surgenor smiled to himself as he stepped into the jetting warmth of the shower cubicle. 'There aren't any towels up here,' he called. 'Can you bring me one—'

A minute later Julie came into the bathroom with a towel. She was wearing a yellow robe, loosely tied, and her gold hair was drawn back with a gold ribbon. The beauty of her filled Surgenor's eyes.

'I was sure . . .' Julie stopped speaking as she glanced around the bathroom and saw the plenitude of towels on their rails. 'Oh, Dave! What's the idea of bringing me all the way upstairs?'

Surgenor grinned at her. 'Can't you guess?'

She ran her gaze over his taut body. 'The coffee's ready.'

'Not as ready as I am. Come on in – the water's lovely.'

'Promise not to get my hair wet?' she said, pretending the reluctance which was only a part of their love games.

'I promise.'

Julie untied her robe, let it slide back from her shoulders and on to the floor. She stepped into the shower with him. Surgenor took her in his arms and in the minutes that followed he purged himself of all the desire, all the loneliness that a spaceflier is fated to accumulate during his wanderings.

Later, as they were seated at the breakfast table, he felt a strange

43

thought growing unbidden in his mind: *If I'm an architect, if I really am an architect, how can I know so much about the way a spaceman feels?*

He stared at Julie in a kind of sad puzzlement, and became aware of a soft pressure at the back of his neck. It felt exactly like a pillow. He raised his head, blinked uncomprehendingly at the sparse furnishings of his room in the *Sarafand*'s living quarters, then threw the pillow aside. Underneath was the flat silvery disc of a Trance-Port player.

Surgenor picked the disc up and one part of his mind tried to solve the mystery of its presence, while another part which felt hurt and betrayed thought: *Julie, Julie, why couldn't you have been real?*

He dressed as quickly as he could, left his room and had almost reached the companionway down to the mess when he felt himself being pushed aside. Turning back indignantly he saw Victor Voysey, whose face was angry and abnormally pale. Surgenor began to protest, then he noticed the other man was also carrying a Trance-Port tape player.

'What's the matter, Vic?' he said, his mind still blurred with the images of the night.

'Somebody switched tapes on me, that's what's the matter. And I'll kill the bastard when I find out who he is.' Voysey was breathing heavily.

'Switched tapes on you?'

'That's what I said. Somebody went into my room and took my own tape and put a different one in the player.'

Surgenor felt the coolness of premonition. 'What tape did you get? Could you recognize it?'

'I think it was young Hilliard's. The girl seemed . . .' Voysey stopped speaking as he noticed the disc in Surgenor's hand. 'What's going on here, Dave? I thought you didn't use them?'

'I don't – but the joker slipped one under my pillow anyway.'

'Then it must have been mine.'

'No. It was Hilliard's.'

Voysey looked baffled. 'But there should be only one of each.'

'So I'm told.' Surgenor went down the companionway into the mess room, followed by Voysey. Most of the crew were already there, standing in a knot at the 'east' end of the room, but Surgenor's gaze was drawn to the scattering of silvery discs on the table. His premonition crystallized into angry certainty.

'Hi, Dave, Victor,' Pollen said. 'I see you've been done as well – welcome to the club.'

'How did you like the gang bang?' Gillespie asked, chuckling.

Lamereux glared at him, his brown eyes rimmed with white. 'This isn't funny, Al. I don't use tapes, but somebody went into my room, into my *head* – and I don't like it.'

'If everybody got the same tape sequence, then somebody must have taken Bernie Hilliard's tape from his room and made a dozen or so copies.'

'I thought the cassettes were designed to prevent copying.'

'They are, but a man with the right experience could do it.'

'Who?'

Surgenor glanced around the room. One man had stayed apart from the discussion and was seated at the table, studiously unconcerned, taking a platter of ham and eggs from the dispensing turret. Surgenor went over to him, with the others following.

'You went too far, Barrow,' Surgenor said.

Barrow raised his eyebrows in polite surprise. 'I've no idea what you're talking about, old son.'

'You know, all right. Leaving aside the whole invasion of privacy bit, I'm going to report you for maliciously starting a fire on board ship. You'll do time for that.'

'Me!' Barrow looked indignant. 'I never started any fire. Why should I?'

'To get everybody down in the hangar so that you could steal Bernie's Trance-Port and copy the tape and slip it into all the rooms.'

'You're crazy,' Barrow sneered. 'I'm going to excuse it this time, but next time you make an accusation like that, get yourself some proof.'

'I'll get proof this time,' Surgenor told him. 'Aesop monitors all our movements, continuously, only it's written into our contracts that the recordings will never be played unless it's a matter of ship safety or a criminal investigation – and this comes under both those headings. I'll call Aesop now.'

'Wait a minute!' Barrow stood up, spread his hands and put on

45

one of his slate-grey smiles. 'I'm no criminal, for God's sake. Can't you guys take a joke?'

'*Joke!*' Voysey pushed by Surgenor and grabbed two handfuls of Barrow's shirt. 'What did you do with my tape?'

'I put it away safe for you. Take it easy, will you?' Barrow had begun to look nervous.

'Let him go – that doesn't solve anything,' Surgenor said, noting with a sense of surprise that Voysey's main concern seemed to be the safety of his own Trance-Port tape.

Barrow smoothed out his shirt when he was released. 'Look, fellows, I'm sorry if I upset you. It was only . . .'

'What the hell was the idea?' Voysey was not satisfied and his sand-coloured brows were pulled low over his eyes. 'Why did you do it?'

'I . . .' Barrow stopped speaking and a gleam of triumph was kindled in his eyes as Bernie Hilliard came into the room. Hilliard looked pink, relaxed and happy.

'Sorry I'm late, men,' he said. 'I was having such a good time I just didn't want to wake up this morning. What's going on here, any-way?' He allowed his gaze to travel curiously around the group.

'Something you ought to know about,' Voysey rumbled. 'Our shipmate Barrow, here . . .'

Surgenor caught his arm. 'Wait a minute, Vic.'

Voysey shook himself free impatiently. '. . . went into your room yesterday, took your Trance-Port, made a dozen copies of it and slipped it under all our pillows. We all got it last night. That's what's going on here, Bernie.'

Hilliard flinched as though he had been struck and the colour faded from his cheeks. He stared at Barrow, who was nodding eagerly, and then turned to Surgenor.

'Is this true, Dave?'

'It's true.' Surgenor looked into the boy's eyes, thought of Julie as she moved her nakedness against him beneath the warm jets, and turned his gaze away, feeling guilty and embarrassed. Hilliard looked around the rest of the group, shaking his head and moving his lips. The others shuffled their feet, unwilling to face him.

'I did you all a favour,' Barrow said. 'A girl like that Julie *ought* to be public property.'

Voysey stepped behind Barrow and, with an abrupt movement,

pinned his arms. 'Come on, kid,' he said to Hilliard. 'Wreck his face. Get my axle wrench and pulp him up – he deserves it.'

Barrow struggled to get free, but Voysey held him easily while a bleak-eyed Hilliard moved closer and bunched his knuckles. Surgenor knew he should intervene, yet found himself unwilling to do so. Hilliard measured his distance with ritual slowness, drew back his fist, hesitated, and then turned away.

Voysey pleaded with him. 'Come on, kid – you're *entitled*!'

'Why should I?' Hilliard's lips stretched into a smile which was anything but a smile. 'Tod's right in what he says – a guy would be real mean if he didn't want to share a good whore with his friends.'

But Julie's not like that! The protest was in Surgenor's mind, and he had almost spoken it, when he realized he was on the verge of making a fool of himself. They were not talking about a real woman, dressed in yellow and gold, who had sat with him at breakfast and smiled with the sharing of memories. The subject under discussion was only a complex of patterns on a magnetic tape.

'Let the man go,' Hilliard said, taking a seat at the table. 'Now, what's for breakfast? After the night I had I need some solid nourishment inside me. Know what I mean?' He winked at the man nearest to him. Surgenor looked at Hilliard with a sudden and irrational dislike, then turned back to Barrow.

'You're not getting away with this,' Surgenor said, and – filled with a rage he did not want to acknowledge or understand – walked away from the mess table and headed for the solitude of his room.

'Hear these words.'

'I'm listening to you, David.'

Surgenor lay still on his bed, trying to marshal his thoughts. 'I'm reporting to you, officially, that the fire on the hangar deck yesterday was started by Tod Barrow. Deliberately. He has just admitted to doing it.' Surgenor went on to describe the subjective events as objectively as he could.

'I see,' Aesop commented when he had finished. 'Do you think there will be more trouble between Barrow and Hilliard?'

'I . . .' Surgenor considered building another case for aborting the mission, but similar arguments had always failed with Aesop. 'I don't think there'll be any more trouble. It seems to me they've burned themselves out.'

'Thank you, David.' There was a brief silence, then Aesop said, 'You will be interested to learn that I have decided to terminate the mission. That means you can be back on Earth before the twenty-fifth of December, as you wished.'

'What?'

'You will be interested to learn that I have ...'

'Don't go over it again – I got you.' Surgenor sat up on the bed, almost afraid to believe what he had heard. 'What made you change your mind?'

'The circumstances have changed.'

'In what way?'

There was another silence. 'Barrow is more unpredictable than you think, David.'

'Go on.'

'He has interfered with my memory and logic. In my judgement it is necessary for me to return to the nearest regional HQ so that certain readjustments, which are beyond my capabilities, can be carried out as soon as possible.'

'Aesop, I don't understand you.' Surgenor stared at the speaker grille on the wall. 'What did Barrow actually do?'

'He made an extra copy of Hilliard's Trance-Port tape and fed it into one of my data inputs.'

The words were almost an obscenity to Surgenor. 'But ... I didn't think that sort of thing was possible.'

'It is possible to a properly qualified man. In the future the Cartographical Service will place an upper limit on the amount of experience survey crew members have in certain fields. Also, they will probably discontinue the Trance-Port experiment.'

'This is weird,' Surgenor said, still trying to grasp the full implications of what he had been told. 'I mean, was the tape even compatible with your internal languages?'

'To a large extent. I am very versatile, which in this case represents an area of vulnerability. For example, I have decided to abort this mission ... but I am not entirely certain that my decision is based on pure logic.'

'It seems perfectly logical to me – somebody as dangerous as Barrow needs treatment as soon as possible.'

'Correct, but the fact that I am alert to him vastly reduces his potential for harm. It may be that I now understand your desire to return to your home, and that I am being influenced by it in a non-logical manner.'

'That's highly unlikely, Aesop. Believe me, this is one subject on which I'm better informed than you.' Surgenor got to his feet and walked to the door of his room. 'Do you mind if I break the news to the men before you speak to them?'

'I have no objection, as long as you do not discuss the real reasons for the decision.'

'I won't.' Surgenor was opening the door when Aesop spoke again. 'David, before you go ...' the disembodied voice was strangely hesitant '... the data on Hilliard's tape ... is it an accurate portrayal of the human male–female relationship?'

'It is highly idealized,' Surgenor said slowly, 'but it can be like that.'

'I see. Do you think Julie really exists somewhere?'

'No. Only on tape.'

'David, to me everything exists only on tape.'

'I can't help you, Aesop.' Surgenor looked around the metal walls, behind every one of which were the myriad copper skeins of Aesop's nervous system, and he felt a curious emotion. Pity compounded with distaste. He tried to think of something relevant and meaningful to say, but the words which emerged were trite and utterly incongruous.

'You had better forget her.'

'Thank you for the advice,' Aesop said, 'but I have the perfect memory.'

That's tough, Surgenor thought as he closed the door of his room behind him and hurried in the direction of the mess with the good news.

Already, as is the way with human beings, the images of Julie Cornwallis were fading from his mind, to be replaced by pleasurable thoughts about the precious fleeting afternoons of winter on Earth, about football matches and cigar stores and women at supper tables, and about the deep comforts of families drawing together at Christmas.

five

Mike Targett stared morosely into the forward view screens of *Module Five*. The vehicle was travelling at a height of one metre – and at its maximum survey speed – across a flat brown desert. Apart from the plume of dust which rolled constantly in the rear screen, there was no sign of movement anywhere on the broad face of Horta VII. And no sign of life.

'Eight dead worlds in succession,' he grumbled. 'Why do we never find life?'

'Because we work for the Cartographical Service,' Surgenor told him, shifting to a more comfortable position in the module's other seat. 'If this was an inhabited world we wouldn't be allowed to buzz all over it like this.'

'I know that, but I'd like to feel there was some chance of making contact with somebody. Anybody.'

'I would suggest,' Surgenor said peacefully, 'that you join the Diplomatic Service.' He closed his eyes, with every appearance of a man about to drift into a contented after-dinner sleep.

'What are the qualifications? All I know is survey work and a bit of astronomy.'

'You've got the main one – the ability to talk for a long time without saying much.'

'Thanks.' Targett glanced resentfully at the older man's relaxed profile. He had a growing respect for Surgenor and his lengthy experience in the Service, but at the same time he was not sure if he wanted to emulate Surgenor's career. It took a special kind of mind to withstand an endless succession of treks across bleak alien globes, and Targett was almost sure he did not have it. The thought of growing old in the Service filled him with a cool dismay that strengthened his resolve to make some money quickly and get out while he was young enough to enjoy spending it. He had even decided where he would have his big fling.

Next furlough he was going to visit Earth and try his luck on some of the legendary race courses there. A gambler had no trouble finding gaming facilities on any of the Federation's inhabited worlds, but horse racing was a different matter – and actually to stand on the historic turf of Santa Anita or Ascot . . .

'Dave,' he said wistfully, 'weren't you in the Service in the old days when they used to allow the modules to break the search pattern and race back to the ship for the last five hundred kilometres?'

Surgenor's eyes flickered. 'The old days? That was only a couple of years ago.'

'That's the old days in this business.'

'We used to race back to the ship, but it led to trouble once and they introduced a regulation specifically forbidding it.' Surgenor spoke amiably enough, but it was obvious that he wanted to concentrate on going to sleep.

'Did you make any money out of it?' Targett persisted.

'How?'

'By laying odds on the winner.'

'It wouldn't have worked.' Surgenor yawned theatrically, making his point about not wanting to talk. 'Every module had exactly the same chance – one in six.'

'Not *exactly* the same chance,' Targett said warming to his subject. 'I happen to know that Aesop tolerates a dispersion of up to thirty kilometres when he's setting the *Sarafand* down at a pole – and if it worked out right at both ends one module could have a sixty-kilometre advantage over its opposite number. All you would have to do to set up a profitable book would be ...'

'Mike,' Surgenor interrupted tiredly, 'did you ever stop to consider that if you poured all that ingenuity into a legitimate business enterprise you'd be so rich you wouldn't need to gamble?'

Targett was appalled. 'What has being rich or not being rich got to do with gambling?'

'I thought that was why you did it – to make money.'

'Go back to sleep, Dave – I'm sorry I disturbed you.' Targett rolled his eyes skyward and settled down to scowling at the forward screen again. A range of low hills had appeared about ten kilometres to the right, but otherwise the brown deserts of Horta VII were as featureless as ever. He had been slumped in his seat for a quarter of an hour when the module's computer – which was actually a sub-unit of Aesop – made an announcement.

'Receiving atypical data,' it droned. 'Receiving atypical data.'

*

'Computer Five, give details,' Targett said, nudging Surgenor and finding that the big man had already wakened as though by instinct.

'At a bearing of two-six and a range of eight-two kilometres there are a number of metallic objects on the planetary surface. They are approximately seven metres in length. First estimate of number of objects is three-six-three. Concentration and consistency of metallic elements indicate refining. Analysis of reflected radiation indicates machine-finished exteriors.'

Targett's heart began a slow, steady pounding. 'Did you hear that, Dave? What do you think it means?'

'It sounds to me as though you've got your wish – those can't be anything but artifacts.' Surgenor's voice betrayed no excitement but Targett noticed he was now sitting upright as he made a bearing check. 'According to the reading they must be in those hills over there on the right.'

Targett scanned the slowly unfolding slopes which trembled in the heat haze created by Horta. 'It looks pretty dead over there.'

'The whole planet is dead – otherwise Aesop would have noticed something during the preliminary orbital survey.'

'Well, let's go over and take a look.'

Surgenor shook his head. 'Aesop won't agree to our breaking the search pattern unless there's an emergency. It distorts his world map, and as far as a CS ship is concerned the map is the most important factor in nearly any situation.'

'*What?*' Targett wriggled impatiently in his seat. 'I don't give a damn about the world map. Are we supposed to ride straight on and ignore a real archaeological find? I tell you, Dave, if you or Aesop or anybody else thinks that I'm going to . . .' He stopped speaking as he noticed Surgenor's smile. 'You got me going again, didn't you?'

'I guess so – it's hard to resist it with you,' Surgenor said looking complacent. 'Don't worry about us passing up a find. We aren't meant to be archaeologists, but there's a provision in survey regulations for this kind of thing. As soon as we get back to the *Sarafand* Captain Aesop will send a couple of modules out again for a closer look.'

'A couple of modules? Everybody won't be in on it?'

'If Aesop thinks it's important he might bring the ship down here.'

'But this has *got* to be important.' Targett gestured helplessly

52

towards the hills drifting by on his right. 'Hundreds of machine-finished articles just lying on the surface. What could they be?'

'Who knows? My guess is that a ship put down here, possibly for repairs, and dumped a load of unwanted canisters.'

'Oh?' Such a prosiac explanation had not occurred to Targett, and he fought to conceal his disappointment. 'Recently?'

'Depends on what you mean by recent. The *Sarafand* was the first Federation ship to enter the Horta system – and it's been seven thousand years or more since the old White Empire withdrew from this region, so . . .'

'Seven thousand years!'

Targett experienced a brief headiness strangely reminiscent of that sensation which had only once before come over him – the time he had brought off an eight-throw antimartingale on the gaming tables of Parador. This was a new and more satisfactory form of gambling – one in which a man staked lonely hours of boredom as he skimmed across the surfaces of dead worlds, and the prize was a sudden clear look at reality, a handshake from the ghost of an alien being who had been computing his way across the graviton tides of space before the pyramids were planned. Unexpectedly, and for the first time, Targett was glad he had signed on with the Cartographical Service – but a new worry was making itself felt. Suppose he was not among the group Aesop was going to send back to investigate the find?

'Dave,' he said carefully, 'how will Aesop select the modules he wants to come back here?'

'Like a computer.' Surgenor gave a wry smile. 'For an unscheduled foray he likes to use the modules which have clocked up the least engine hours – and this old bus is due for . . .'

'Don't tell me – a complete overhaul next month.'

'Next week.'

'That's just great,' Targett said bitterly. 'Two modules out of six. Odds of only two to one against me and I couldn't even bring it off. With my luck I'd . . .' He fell silent as he saw the slow grin spreading over Surgenor's features.

'May I make a suggestion?' Surgenor kept his gaze straight ahead. 'Instead of sitting around here calculating odds, why don't you get suited up and take a walk over into those hills? That way . . .'

'*What*? Can you do things like that?'

Surgenor sighed in the way he always did when a new crew member displayed ignorance. 'I would also suggest that you read the survey regulations when you get back. Each suit is fitted out for an EVA of up to fifty hours for precisely this sort of situation.'

'Skip all that stuff, Dave – I can bone up on regulations later.' Targett's mounting excitement overrode his respect for Surgenor's greater experience. 'Will Aesop clear me to leave the module and take a look at ... whatever it is over there?'

'He ought to – the logistics make sense. You could give him television coverage and a verbal report while I'm taking this module back to the ship in pattern with the others. Only one module would need to return to pick you up. And if the report you turn in shows the find is worth bringing the *Sarafand* down for, there'll be no extra time on the modules at all.'

'Let's talk to Aesop right now.'

'You're sure you want to do this, Mike?' Surgenor's eyes had become serious, probing. 'I'll feel responsible for you all on your own out there, and the Cartographical Service has an occupational disease all to itself – there's a tendency for us to start thinking a planet is just a series of pretty pictures on a screen.'

'What are you getting at?'

'We're so used to coasting around in armchairs that we forget we rely on a machine to transport us around like invalids. It means that no amount of *thinking* about a ten-kilometre walk can prepare you for the actual experience. That's why Aesop hasn't already taken the initiative and ordered one of us to investigate those objects – the Service doesn't require a man to walk new ground alone.'

Targett snorted and pressed the talk button which would put him into direct contact with Aesop.

six

Module Five lifted a short distance into the air, dipped its nose slightly and whined away to the north in a cloud of brown dust.

Targett watched it vanish, and was mildly surprised at the speed with which all sign of the vehicle's existence was lost in the alien panorama. He took a deep breath of the suit's plastic-smelling air. It was early afternoon and he had about six hours of daylight in hand – ample time to reach the group of metal objects which lay due east at a distance of some ten kilometres. He began to trudge towards the hills, scarcely able to credit the turn of events which had snatched him from the boredom of a routine survey and set him down alone in the middle of a prehistoric landscape.

Horta VII's atmosphere contained no trace of oxygen and the planet had never known any indigenous life, yet Targett found he was unable to keep his eyes from scanning the sand underfoot for shells and insects. Intellectually he could accept that he was traversing a dead world, but on the instinctive and emotional level his consciousness simply rejected the concept. He walked as quickly as he could, going ankle-deep in the fine sand, feeling a little self-conscious each time the holstered ultralaser pistol bumped against his thigh.

'I know you don't need it,' Surgenor had said patiently, 'but it's standard EVA equipment and if you don't wear it you don't leave the vehicle.'

The planet's gravity was close to 1.5G, and by the time Targett neared the hills he was sweating freely in spite of the suit's cooling system. He unbuckled the pistol – which seemed to have maliciously quadrupled its weight – and slung it over his shoulder. The ground was becoming increasingly stony and on reaching the hills he found they were composed largely of naked basaltic rock. He sat down on a smooth outcropping, glad of the chance to rest his legs. When he had sipped some cold water from the tube that nuzzled against his left cheek, he decided to check on his location.

'Aesop,' he said, 'how far am I from the objects?'

'The nearest is nine hundred and twelve metres east of your present position,' Aesop replied without hesitation, drawing on the data continuously fed to him by his own sensors and those in the six converging survey modules.

'Thanks.'

Targett scanned the slope ahead of him. It formed an ill-defined ridge a short distance away. From there he should be able to see the objects, provided they were not buried under the accumulated dust of seventy centuries.

'How are you making out, Mike?' The voice was Surgenor's.

'No problems.' Targett was about to add that he was beginning to understand the difference between looking at images and toiling his way through the actual terrain when it dawned on him that Surgenor had maintained a long radio silence with the deliberate intention of making him feel cut off. No doubt the big man had Targett's interests at heart, but Targett was not going to reveal that he knew he had been too casual and brash about the exploit.

'It's good to get some exercise,' he said. 'I'm enjoying the walk. How about you?'

'I've got decisions to make,' Surgenor said comfortably. 'I'll be back at the *Sarafand* in less than three hours, and the question is whether to eat a pack meal now or wait for a proper steak dinner on board. What would you do, Mike?'

'That's one of those tricky decisions you have to sort out for yourself.' Targett kept his voice level with an effort. This was Surgenor's way of reminding him that by waiting a few hours he could have done his investigating in comfort and on a full stomach. As it was, he was going to spend an uncomfortable night with nothing to keep him going but water and surrogate. Another disconcerting aspect of his situation was that an alien world seemed a hundred times more alien to a man who was on his own.

'You're right – it isn't fair for me to load my problems on to you,' Surgenor said. 'Maybe I'll do things the hard way and try to eat both meals.'

'You're breaking my heart, Dave. See you around.' Targett rose to his feet with a new determination to make his private expedition worth while. He moved up the slope, being careful not to slip on the loose surface stones and dust which cascaded around his ankles at every step. Beyond the ridge the ground levelled out for more than a kilometre before rising sharply to the rocky spine of the hills. The small plateau was bounded to the north and south by tumbled palisades of boulders, almost as if it had been cleared by bulldozers.

And scattered across the level ground – in random groupings – were hundreds of slim black cylinders, the nearest only a few dozen paces from Targett. They were about seven metres in length and tapered at each end, with controlled curvatures which spoke of aerodynamic efficiency. Targett's breathing quickened in a way

56

which had nothing to do with his exertions as it came to him that the alien objects certainly were not discarded canisters, as Surgenor had suggested.

He took the miniature television camera from his belt, plugged it into the suit's powerpack for a few seconds to charge its cells, and aimed it at the nearest cylinders.

'Aesop,' he said, 'I've made visual contact.'

'I'm getting a moderately good picture, Michael,' Aesop replied.

'I'll go closer.'

'Do not move,' Aesop commanded sharply.

Targett froze in the act of taking a step forward. 'What's the matter?'

'Perhaps nothing, Michael.' Aesop was speaking at his normal tempo again. 'The picture I'm receiving from you would suggest that the surfaces of the objects are free of dust. Is this correct?'

'I guess it is.' Targett examined the shining black cylinders, ruefully wondering how he had failed to appreciate their condition. They might have been scattered across the plateau only that morning.

'You guess? Does some visual defect prevent you from being positive?'

'Don't be funny, Aesop – I'm positive. Does it mean that the objects have been dumped here recently?'

'Improbable. Has there been any accretion of dust in the vicinity of each object?'

Targett narrowed his eyes into the brilliantly reflected sunlight and saw that the cylinders were lying in cradles of accumulated dust, the upper edges of which were a few centimetres clear of the black metal. He described what he could see.

'Repellant fields,' Aesop said. 'Still effective after a possible seven thousand years. It is not necessary for you to study these objects any further, Michael. As soon as the planetary survey has been completed I shall bring the *Sarafand* to your location for the purpose of a full investigation. You will now retrace your steps to the foot of the hill and wait there for the ship to arrive.'

'What was the point of me walking all the way out here if I'm not going to do anything?' Targett demanded. He thought briefly about

the possible consequences of disobeying a direct order from Aesop –
official reprimands, loss of pay, suspension from duties – then came
to a decision.

'In view of the circumstances, I have no intention of cooling my
heels for four or five hours.' Targett made his voice firm, although
he was uncertain of how good Aesop was at interpreting inflexions.
'I'm going to take a closer look at these things.'

'I will permit that, provided you continue to supply unin-
terrupted television coverage.'

Targett almost pointed out that, with thousands of kilometres
separating them, the computer had no way of imposing its will on
him, but he suppressed his irritation. During his months in the
Service he had managed to swallow the fact that his crewmates
sometimes addressed the ship's computer as 'Captain' and obeyed
its every instruction as though a three-star general was standing over
them in person. The idea of being remotely controlled like a puppet
was more than a little irksome, but there was no point in blowing up
about it just when something of genuine interest had come along to
break the monotonous routine.

'Setting off now,' Targett said. He crossed the level ground,
keeping the camera trained ahead, and as he walked something
about the general appearance of the cylinders began to disturb him.
They looked like military supplies. Torpedoes, perhaps.

The same thought must have occurred to Aesop. 'Michael, have
you made a polyrad check of the area?'

'Yes.' Targett had not, but he held up his left wrist as he spoke,
examined the suit's polyrad dial and saw it was registering nothing
unusual. He moved the dial into camera view for a second, giving
proof there were no nuclear warheads in the area.

'Clean as a whistle. Do these things look like torpedoes to you,
Aesop?'

'They could be anything. Proceed carefully.'

Targett, who had been proceeding anyway, clamped his mouth
shut and tried to put Aesop out of his mind. He approached the
nearest cylinder, marvelling at its gleaming electrostatic freshness.

'Hold the camera one metre from the object,' Aesop said in-
trusively. 'Walk slowly around it and return to your starting point.'

'Yes, *sir*,' Targett muttered, moving crab-wise around the cylinder. One end of it tapered almost to a point, culminating in a

one-centimetre circular hole which reminded him of the muzzle of a rifle. A ring of black glass, practically indistinguishable from the surrounding metal, was located a handsbreadth back from the point. The other end of the cylinder was more rounded and was covered with similar holes rather like those on a pepper shaker. In the object's mid-section were several plates set flush with the surface and secured by screws which might have been made on Earth except that their slots were Y-shaped. There were no markings of any kind.

As he completed the circuit Targett was once again stirred by the sheer wonder of the experience of being so close to an artifact from a vanished civilization. He made a guilty resolution to obtain a souvenir and smuggle it on to the ship if the opportunity presented itself. *Better still*, he thought, *a boxful of parts would fetch a good price from a dealer in . . .*

'Thank you, Michael,' Aesop said. 'I have recorded details of the object's exterior – now see if you can remove the plates from the centre section.'

'Right.'

Targett was mildly surprised at Aesop's instruction, but he set the camera down where it could cover his actions and unsheathed his knife.

'Just a minute, Mike,' Surgenor's voice cut in, unexpectedly loud and clear in spite of hundreds of kilometres which now lay between Targett and *Module Five*. 'You mentioned torpedoes a minute ago. What do those things actually look like?'

'Dave,' Targett said wearily, 'why don't you go back to your pack meal?'

'I've got indigestion – now tell me what you've got there.'

Targett described the cylinders quickly and with a growing feeling of exasperation. His projected stroll down the centuries, among the relics of a long-gone extraterrestrial culture, was somehow getting him more tangled than ever in the petty restrictions of the present.

'Do you mind if I get on with the job?' he concluded.

'I don't think you should touch those things, Mike.'

'Why not? They look like torpedoes – but if there was any chance of one of them blowing up Aesop would have warned me off.'

'Would he?' Surgenor's voice was hard. 'Don't forget that Aesop is a computer . . .'

'You don't need to tell *me* that – you're one of the people who personalize him.'

'. . . and therefore thinks in a very logical manner. Didn't you notice his sudden change in attitude just now? At first he wanted you to stay clear of the objects – now he's telling you to take one apart.'

'Which proves he thinks it's safe,' Targett said.

'Which proves he thinks it could be dangerous, you bonehead. Listen, Mike, this little jaunt of yours has turned out rather different from what any of us expected and, since you were the one who volunteered to go out on the limb, Aesop is quite prepared to let you saw it off behind you.'

Targett shook his head, although there was nobody there to see him. 'If Aesop thought there was any risk he would order me away from here.'

'Let's ask him,' Surgenor snapped. 'Aesop, why did you instruct Mike to remove the casing from one of those cylinders?'

'To permit inspection of its interior,' Aesop replied.

Surgenor sighed audibly. 'Sorry. What was the reasoning behind your permitting Mike to proceed with this investigation alone instead of waiting for the arrival of the customary two modules or the entire ship?'

'The objects in question resemble torpedoes or missiles or bombs,' Aesop replied without hesitation, 'but the complete absence of electrical or mechanical interfaces on their surfaces suggests that they may be self-contained automatic devices. Their contamination repellant systems are still active, so there is a possibility that other systems are either active or capable of being activated. If the objects prove to be robot weapons it is obviously better that they be examined by one man rather than by four or twelve – especially as that man has refused a direct order to leave the area and therefore has limited the Cartographical Service's legal responsibilities and obligations.'

'QED,' Surgenor commented drily. 'There you are, Mike. Captain Aesop firmly believes in pursuing the greatest good of the greatest number. And in this case you're the smallest number.'

'I cannot risk the ship,' Aesop said.

'He can't risk the ship, Mike. Now that you know the score, you are entitled to refuse to chance going near those objects until a team arrives with full probe instrumentation.'

'I don't think there's any risk worth mentioning,' Targett said steadily. 'Besides, everything Aesop said makes sense to me – it's only reasonable to play the odds. I'm going ahead.'

Analysing his own feelings, Targett was surprised to discover that he was slightly disappointed in Aesop. He had always objected to the way in which his shipmates tended to personalize the computer, yet in his heart he must have regarded Aesop as a benign entity who could be relied on to look out for Targett's welfare with greater scrupulousness than could have been expected of a human skipper. Possibly there was something there a psychoanalyst could get his teeth into, but his immediate concern was with the interior of the nearest cylinder. He unclipped the heavy backpack, set it on the ground and kneeled beside the sleek black torpedo-shape.

The Y-slots in the screws holding the mid-section plates did not provide a good purchase for his knife, but the crews proved to be spring-loaded and turned easily when depressed. He lifted the first plate off carefully, exposing a mass of components and circuitry, much of which appeared to be duplicated and arranged symmetrically about a flat central spine. The wires and conduits were drab and without colour coding, but looked fresh enough to have been installed weeks and not millennia earlier.

Targett, who had no engineering background beyond what he had picked up in the CS course, suddenly felt a profound respect for the long-departed beings who had created the cylinders. Within five minutes he had stripped off all the curved plates and laid them in a row beside the cylinder body. An inspection of the complex interior told him nothing about the object's function, but the mechanism in the sharper end had the hard uncompromising lines he associated with machine guns.

'Again hold the camera one metre from the object and move along its entire length,' Aesop instructed. 'Then return with the camera held in such a way as to give me close-ups of the interior compartments.'

Targett did as he had been told, pausing at what he had come to regard as the rear end. 'How's that? This looks like an engine section, but the metal looks queer – a bit crumbly.'

'That would be caused by nitrogen absorption associated with ...' Aesop stopped speaking in mid-sentence, a strangely human mannerism which caused Targett to prick his ears.

'Aesop?'

'Here is an instruction you must obey instantly.' Aesop's voice was preternaturally sharp. 'Scan your surroundings. If you see a rock formation that would give protection against machine rifle fire – *go to it immediately!*'

'But what's the matter?' Targett glanced around the shimmering plateau.

'Don't ask questions,' Surgenor's voice cut in. 'Do as Aesop says, Mike – run for cover!'

'But . . .'

Targett's voice faded as his peripheral vision picked up a sudden movement. He turned towards it and saw that – in the centre of the plateau – one of the hundreds of cylinders had reared its sharp end at an angle into the air and was swaying, slowly, menacingly, like a cobra hypnotizing its intended victim.

seven

Targett gaped at the cylinder for a moment, his face contorted with shock, then he ran north towards the nearest barricade of rock. Hampered by the suit and the extra gravity, he found it impossible to pick up any real speed. On his right the cylinder spiralled lazily into the air like a mythological creature awakening from millennia of slumber. It drifted in his direction.

Two others stirred in their dusty cradles.

Targett tried to move faster, but felt as if he was waist-deep in molasses. Ahead he saw a black triangular hole formed by tilted slabs of rock, and he swerved towards it.

The sky to his right was clear again, giving him the impression the airborne cylinder had vanished. Then he saw it moving around behind him, foreshortening, aiming itself. His thighs pumped harder in nightmarish slow motion and the dark opening swung crazily ahead, but too far away. He knew he was going to be too late.

He threw himself at the opening – just as a massive hammer-blow sledged ferociously into his back. The television camera spun from his hand as he was lifted off his feet and flung into the space between the rocks. Astounded at finding himself still alive, Targett burrowed desperately for cover. The triangular space proved long enough to take his whole body. He squirmed into it, sobbing with panic at the thought of another bullet finding him at any instant.

I'm alive, he thought numbly. *But how?*

He slid a gloved hand around to the lower part of his back where the bullet had struck, and felt an unfamiliar jagged edge of metal. His probing fingers explored a crumpled, box-like object, and a few more seconds passed before he identified it as the ruins of his oxygen generator unit.

He started to reach for the backpack containing the spare generator, then remembered the pack was lying out on the plateau where he had set it down before going to work on the cylinder. Clawing feverishly at the confining rock until he had reversed his position, he peered outside. The small segment of open sky he could see was being crossed and re-crossed by the black silhouettes of torpedoes in flight.

Targett inched forward a little for a better view. His eyes widened as he saw that the torpedoes had taken to the air in hundreds, swarming silently upwards, their shadows rippling over the brownish dust and rocks. Even as he watched, a few laggards angled their noses into the air, swung groggily for a moment and drifted up to join their fellows in the circulating cloud. A slight fold in the ground made it impossible for him to see where the backpack lay, or if the cylinder on which he had worked had also taken flight. He raised his head slightly and fell back amid a blasting shower of rock splinters and dust. The banshee howl of ricochets left no doubt in his mind that several of the torpedoes had noted his movements and had reacted in the only way they could, according to the lethal dictates of their ancient designers.

'Report on your position, Michael,' Aesop's voice seemed to come from another existence.

'My position isn't so good,' Targett said hoarsely, trying to control his breathing. 'These things seem to be robot hunters fitted out with machine rifles. The lot of them are airborne right now – it might be that the radiation from my camera or suit radio triggered them off – and they're swarming about like mosquitoes. I'm hiding out under some rocks, but . . .'

'Stay where you are. I will have the *Sarafand* there in less than an hour.'

'That's no good, Aesop. One of the torpedoes took a shot at me as I was getting in here. The suit isn't punctured, but my oxygenerator is wrecked.'

'Use the spare from your pack,' Surgenor put in before Aesop could reply.

'I can't.' Targett made the strange discovery that he felt embarrassed rather than afraid. 'The pack's lying out in the open and I can't get at it. There's no way for me to get it.'

'But that gives you only . . .' Surgenor paused. 'You'll have to reach the pack, Mike.'

'That's what I was thinking.'

'Look, perhaps the torpedoes respond only to sudden movement. If you crawled out very slowly . . .'

'Hypothesis incorrect,' Aesop interrupted. 'My analysis of the sensor circuitry in the torpedo which Michael opened indicates that it was a duplex system, both channels of which use movement and heat for target identification. Any exposure of his body would be certain to draw more fire.'

'It already has – I tried to poke my head out of this hole a minute ago,' Targett said. 'I almost got it blown off.'

'That shows my conclusion about the sensor circuitry was correct, which in turn . . .'

'We haven't time to listen to you congratulating yourself, Aesop.' Surgenor's voice crashed in the suit's radio. 'Mike, have you tried your sidearm on them?'

Targett reached for the ultralaser, which was still slung over his shoulder, then pulled his hand back. 'It wouldn't help, Dave. There are hundreds of those things buzzing around out there, and an ultralaser pistol holds – how many charges?'

'Let's see . . . If it's one of the capsule-powered jobs there should be twenty-six.'

'So what's the point in even trying?'

'Maybe there isn't any point, Mike, but are you just going to lie there and suffocate? Blast a few of them just for the hell of it.'

'David Surgenor,' Aesop came in forcibly, 'I instruct you to remain silent while I deal with this emergency.'

'Deal with it?' Targett felt an illogical stirring of his former blind faith in Aesop. 'All right, Aesop. What do you want me to do?'

'Can you see any of the torpedoes without endangering yourself?'

'Yes.' Targett glanced at the triangular area of sky as a black cigar-shape drifted across it. 'Only one at a time, though.'

'That is sufficient. Your record shows that you are an adequate marksman. I want you to use your sidearm on one of the torpedoes. Hit it near the nose section.'

'What's the point?' Targett's brief, irrational hope dissolved into raw anger and panic. 'I've got twenty-six charges and there are three hundred of those robots out there.'

'Three hundred and sixty-two to be precise,' Aesop said. 'Now listen to my instructions and obey them without further delay. Direct an ultralaser burst against one of the torpedoes. Hit as close to the nose section as is possible without jeopardizing the shot and describe the effects of your action.'

'You smug . . .' Realizing the futility of trying to insult the computer, Targett wrenched the pistol free of its holster and flipped the tubeless scopesight up into position.

He set the sight for low magnification and wriggled around in the narrow space between the rocks until he was in a reasonably good firing attitude. The controlled breathing essential for high-accuracy shooting was impossible – his lungs were working like bellows in the suit's stale air – but the torpedoes were a relatively easy target for a radiation weapon. He waited until one came questing across his segment of sky, put the cross-hairs on its conical nose section and squeezed the trigger. As the first capsule in the weapon's magazine yielded its energy, a quarter-second burst of violet brilliance lanced out, flaring briefly on the torpedo's nose. The black cylinder seemed to falter slightly, then it recovered and cruised out of sight, apparently unharmed.

Targett felt perspiration prickling out on his forehead. Incredible as it seemed, he – Michael Targett, the most important individual in the universe – was going to die, just like all the anonymous beings who had gone before him.

'I hit one,' he said through numb lips. 'Right on the nose. It just flew on as if nothing had happened.'

'Was there any searing or scarring of metal?'

'I don't think so. I'm seeing them in silhouette, so I couldn't be very sure, though.'

'You say the torpedo flew on as though nothing had happened,' Aesop persisted. 'Think carefully, Michael – was there no reaction at all?'

'Well, it seemed to wobble for a fraction of a second, but ...'

'Just as I expected,' Aesop commented. 'The internal arrangement of the torpedo you examined suggested it had a duplex sensory and control system. The new evidence confirms this.'

'Damn you, Aesop,' Targett whispered. 'I thought you were trying to help me, but you were just gathering more data. From now on, do your own dirty work – I've retired from the Service.'

'The ultralaser radiation would have been sufficient to burn out the prime sensory inputs,' Aesop continued, unperturbed, 'causing the back-up system to take over. Another direct hit on the same torpedo would make it fall out of control, and the probability is that the impact would cause catastrophic failure of the motor casing, which appears to have deteriorated with time.

'The high level of non-directional radiation associated with a failure in a motor of this design should in turn be sufficient to overload both sensory channels in the other torpedoes, causing them ...'

'It could work!' Targett felt a sun-bright pang of relief – but it faded as quickly as it had been born. He fought to keep his emotions hidden from any listeners, and especially Dave Surgenor.

'The only trouble is I could see no mark on the torpedo I hit – and if I try to poke my face out for a better look around I'll get it full of pills. Maybe that would be the best thing that could happen – at least it would be quick.'

'Let me say something here, Aesop,' came Surgenor's voice. 'Listen Mike – you still have a chance. You've got twenty-five capsules left in your magazine. Blast away at the torpedoes as they go by and maybe you'll burn the same one twice.'

'Thanks, Dave.' A grey mood of resignation settled over Targett as he realized what he had to do. 'I appreciate your concern, but remember I'm the gambler in this outfit. Twenty-six into three-sixty-two puts the odds at about thirteen to one against me right at the start. Thirteen's a bad number, and I don't feel very lucky.'

'But if it's your only chance . . .'

'Not the only one.' Targett gathered his legs beneath him in preparation for strenuous action. 'I'm a pretty good shot with radiation weapons. My best bet would be to get outside fast – out where I can track one of the torpedoes long enough to take two shots at it.'

'Don't try it, Mike,' Surgenor said urgently.

'Sorry.' Targett tensed himself and edged forward. 'My mind is . . .'

'Your mind appears to be confused,' Aesop cut in, 'possibly due to oxygen starvation. Have you forgotten that you dropped your television camera outside your shelter?'

Targett hesitated in the act of throwing himself forward. 'The camera? Is it still running? Can you see all of the swarm?'

'Not all of it, but enough to let me follow individual torpedoes for a considerable portion of their circuit. I will instruct you when to fire, and by timing your shots to match the general circulation rate of the swarm we can bring the probability of a second hit on one torpedo close to unity.'

'All right, Aesop – you win.' Targett settled down again, burdened by the dull certainty that nothing he could do would make any difference to the outcome. His breathing had become rapid and shallow as his lungs rejected their own waste products, and his hands were clammy inside the gloves. He raised the sidearm and peered through its sight.

'Begin firing at will to initiate the sequence.' Aesop's voice came faintly through the roaring in Targett's ears.

'Right.' He steadied the weapon, waited until a torpedo drifted across the triangular patch of sky, and directed a burst of energy on to its nose section. The torpedo wavered for an instant, then flew on. Targett repeated the process again and again, always with the same result, until the pile of expended capsules spat out by the weapon numbered more than a dozen.

'Where are you, Aesop?' he breathed. 'You're not helping me.'

'The ultralaser radiation leaves no visible marks on the surfaces of the torpedoes, so I am forced to work on a purely statistical basis,' Aesop said. 'But I now have sufficient data to enable me to predict their movements with a suitable degree of accuracy.'

'Then start doing it, for God's sake.'

There was a slight pause. 'Each time I say "now" fire at the next torpedo appearing in your field of view.'

'I'm waiting.' Targett blinked to clear his vision. Bright-rimmed black spots had begun to dance across it.

'Now.'

A torpedo appeared an instant later and Targett squeezed the trigger. The ultralaser ray raked along the nose section – but after an initial tremor the black cylinder drifted steadily out of view without changing direction.

'Now.'

Targett fired again, with the same result.

'Now.'

Once again the beam of energy flicked across a torpedo – with no serious effect.

'This isn't working out too well.' Targett focused his eyes with difficulty on the indicator on the butt of the pistol. 'I'm down to eight charges. I'm beginning to think ... to think I ought to go ahead with my own plan while I ...'

'You are wasting time, Michael. Now.'

Targett squeezed the trigger and another torpedo drifted heedlessly on, effectively unharmed.

'Now.'

Hopelessly, Targett fired again. The torpedo had passed out of sight before it dawned on him that perhaps it had begun to change direction.

'Aesop,' he managed to say, 'I think maybe ...'

He heard a dull explosion and the triangular segment of sky turned a blinding white. Only the immediate darkening of his helmet's face plate saved Targett's eyes from the full fury of the motor's self-annihilation. The brilliance continued unabated for seconds as the alien engine consumed itself. He imagined it burning out the primary and back-up sensors on the swarming robots, which would blunder down to the ground or fly into the hillside and ...

Just in time, Targett squeezed his eyes shut and buried his head in his arms while a prolonged cataclysm raged all around him, laying waste to the area. *I can still die,* he thought. *Captain Aesop has done his best for me, but if I'm not lucky – this is where I go down.*

When the extended rumble of explosions and the almost palpable torrent of brilliance had died away, he crawled out from under the rocks and forced his legs to accept his weight. He opened his eyes cautiously. The plateau was littered with inert torpedoes, their motor compartments vaporized. A number of the robot hunters were still airborne, but they paid no attention to him as he ran, weaving drunkenly, towards the spot where he had left the back-pack.

On the way across the plateau the thought occurred to him that one of the torpedoes could have landed right on the pack – something that even Captain Aesop would have been powerless to fore-stall – but he found it lying safely beside the stripped down cylinder, which had not flown. He opened the pack with trembling fingers, took out the spare oxygenerator and experienced a moment of exquisite dread as the ruined generator refused to let itself be detached from the suit's breather hole. With the last dregs of his strength he wrenched it off, clicked the replacement into position and lay down to await the renewal of life.

'Mike?' Surgenor sounded hesitant. 'You all right?'

Targett breathed deeply. 'I'm all right, Dave. Captain Aesop got me out of it.'

'Did you say "Captain"?'

'You heard me.' Targett rose to his feet and surveyed the littered battlefield upon which he and a distant computer had vanquished an enemy host which had lain in wait for seven thousand years. In all probability he would never know what the torpedoes' original pur-pose had been, or why they had been dumped on Horta VII – but his taste for archaeology seemed to have faded. It was sufficient just to be alive in the present. As he scanned the incredible scene one of the torpedoes which was still aloft flew blindly into a ridge two kilometres away. The resultant explosion drenched the plateau with radiance.

Targett flinched away from it. 'There goes another one, Aesop.'

'Your meaning is not clear to me, Michael,' Aesop replied.

'Another torpedo, of course. Didn't you see the flash?'

'No. The televisions camera is not functioning.'

'Oh?' Targett glanced towards his former hiding place, where the camera had fallen. 'Perhaps the light from all those explosions burned something out.'

'No.' Aesop paused. 'Transmissions ceased when you dropped the camera. There is a good probability that the switch got jarred to the off position.'

'Very likely. I was moving at a good . . .' Targett stopped speaking as a disturbing thought occurred to him. 'Then you lied to me. You weren't able to track the torpedoes.'

'Your mental condition made it necessary for me to lie to you.'

'But you were telling me when to fire, for God's sake! How did you know I would hit one of the torpedoes twice?'

'I did not know.' Aesop's voice was precise, unruffled. 'This is something you in particular should understand, Michael. I simply took a chance.'

'This is lovely material for my book, Mike.' Clifford Pollen's reedy voice was pitched with excitement as he leaned across the mess table. 'I'm going to call the chapter "The Day The Targett Started Shooting Back". Good isn't it?'

Mike Targett, who had learned to endure every possible joke about his surname, nodded his head. 'Very original, that.'

Pollen frowned down at his notes. 'I'll have to be careful about how I put the story over, though. There were three-sixty-two torpedoes skimming around and you had only twenty-six shots. That means Aesop staked your life on odds of about one in thirteen – and the gamble came off!'

'Wrong! It wasn't that way, at all.' Targett smiled pityingly as he cut up a medium-rare steak. 'Take my tip and stay away from poker games, Clifford – you've no idea how to calculate odds.'

Pollen looked offended. 'I can perform a simple calculation. Twenty-six into three-sixty-two . . .'

'Has nothing to do with the actual mathematics of the situation, my friend. It was necessary for me to hit one of the torpedoes twice. Right?'

'Right,' Pollen said grudgingly.

'Well, in a situation like that you can't just take simple odds by dividing the smaller number into the larger one the way you did. The reason is that the odds change with every shot. Every time I hit a torpedo I shifted the odds slightly in favour of the following shot, and the only way you can calculate the overall probability is to multiply out twenty-five sets of gradually improving odds. That's pretty hard to do – unless you happen to be a computer – but if you do it you'll get final odds of around two to one that I would hit a torpedo twice. It wasn't much of a gamble really.'

'That's hard to believe.'

'Work it out for yourself with a calculator.' Targett put a square of steak into his mouth and chewed appreciatively. 'It's a good example of the difficulty of judging complex possibilities by common sense.'

Pollen scribbled out some figures. 'It's too complicated for me.'

'That's why you'd never make a successful gambler.'

Targett smiled again as he worked on his steak. He did not mention the fact that his own common sense had been outraged by the mathematics of probability, or that it had taken a long and tedious conversation on a private link with Aesop, after all danger was past, to convince him of the truth. And he would never mention to anyone the feeling of bleak isolation which had stolen over him when he genuinely understood that Aesop – the entity who safe-guarded his life, arranged his meals, and replied patiently to all his questions – was nothing more than a logic machine. It was better to play the same game that all the other crewmen played, to address Aesop as 'Captain' now and then, and to think of him as a superhuman being who never came down from his lonely command post somewhere on the *Sarafand*'s upper decks.

'We'll be putting down on Pandor at the end of this survey,' Dave Surgenor said from the opposite side of the table. 'You'll be able to give us a practical demonstration of successful gambling.'

'I don't think so.' Targett put another forkful of steak into his mouth. 'The syndicates are bound to use computers to calculate the odds. That gives them an unfair advantage.'

eight

The Bubble was the unofficial name given to the expanding volume of space in which every planet and asteroid had been surveyed by men. Some of the worlds examined, the best, were earmarked for colonization or other kinds of development, but only in cases where there was no indigenous civilization. The Cartographical Service's charter empowered it to deal solely with uninhabited planets – all inter-culture contacts being the prerogative of diplomatic or military missions, according to individual circumstances.

As a result of this policy, David Surgenor – although a long-term veteran of the Cartographical Service – had never in the course of his official duties encountered members of an extraterrestrial civilization, and had no expectations of doing so ...

Surgenor stood by without speaking while part of the survey equipment was pulled out of *Module Five* to make room for two extra seats. As soon as the work had been completed he climbed into the heavy vehicle and drove it down the *Sarafand*'s ramp with unnecessary speed. Only a short distance separated the survey ship from the squat bulk of the military vessel *Admiral Carpenter*, but Surgenor selected ground-effect suspension and made the journey amid spectacular plumes of powdery sand. His course was marked by a blood-red gash in the white desert, which slowly healed itself as the phototropic sand returned to its surface.

One of the guards at the foot of the *Admiral Carpenter*'s ramp pointed to where he wanted Surgenor to park and said something into a wrist communicator. Surgenor slid *Module Five* into the indicated slot and killed the lift, allowing the beetle-shaped vehicle to settle on its under surface. He opened the door and the hot, dry air of the planet Saladin gusted into the cabin.

'Major Giyani's party will be with you in two minutes,' the guard called.

Surgenor gave a muted parody of a military salute and slouched further down in his seat. He knew he was behaving childishly, but the *Sarafand* had been grounded on this world for almost a month now – and Surgenor had not been at rest that long in all his years in the Cartographical Service. Waiting in one place, wasting the meagre ration of time granted to humans, had the effect of making him pessimistic and morose. Travel no longer had the same compulsion for him that it used to have, yet he was unable to remain in one place.

He stared resentfully at the sun-blazing white desert which stretched to the horizon and wondered why it had seemed beautiful the first morning he saw it. There had been a wind that day, of course, and its swift-moving patterns had been traced as intricate shadings of crimson-through-white, sweeping across the dunes as buried layers were exposed to the sun and then made their phototropic response to its light.

The *Sarafand* had landed, as always, with the intention of carrying out a routine survey operation. There were obvious difficulties in the terrain, which meant that modules could travel at top speed, and the survey would have been completed in three days had the totally unexpected not occurred.

Three of the module crews had reported seeing apparitions.

The visions had taken two different forms – people and buildings – which shimmered transparently and vanished in a way which would have prompted observers to write them off as mirages – but for the fact that a mirage had to have a physical counterpart somewhere. And an earlier orbital survey of Saladin had established that it was a dead world, containing no intelligent life or traces of its former presence ...

'Waken up, driver,' Major Giyani said crisply. 'We're ready to go.'

Surgenor raised his head with deliberate slowness and eyed the swarthy, black-moustached officer who was standing in the module's entrance and somehow managing to look dapper in regulation battle kit. Behind him was a smooth-faced lieutenant with apologetic blue eyes, and a heavily built sergeant who was carrying a rifle.

'We can't move off until everybody gets in,' Surgenor pointed out reasonably, but in a way which was meant to express his distaste for being treated as a chauffeur. He waited stolidly until the lieutenant and sergeant were in the supernumerary seats in the rear, and the major had sat down in the vacant front seat. The sergeant, whose name Surgenor vaguely remembered as McErlain, did not set his rifle down but cradled it in his lap.

'This is our destination,' Giyani said, handing Surgenor a sheet of paper on which was written a set of grid co-ordinates. 'The straight-line distance from here is about ...'

'Five-hundred-and-fifty kilometres,' Surgenor put in, having performed a rapid mental calculation.

Giyani raised his black eyebrows and looked closely at Surgenor. 'Your name is ... Dave Surgenor, isn't it?'

'Yes.'

'Well then, *Dave*.' Giyani gave a prolonged smile which said, *See how I humour touchy civilians?* – then he pointed at the grid reference. 'Can you get us there by eight-hundred hours, ship time?'

Surgenor decided, too late, that he preferred Giyani when he was being officious. He started the module rolling, switched to ground-effect suspension, and set a course that took them almost due south. There was little conversation during the two-hour journey, but Surgenor noted that Giyani addressed Sergeant McErlain with undisguised dislike, while the lieutenant – whose name was Kelvin – avoided speaking to the barrel-chested man at all. The sergeant answered Giyani in flat monosyllables in a way that remained on the safe side of insolence, but only just. Aware of the charged atmosphere in the module, Surgenor tried to remember the wisps of mess table gossip he had picked up about McErlain, but most of his thoughts were taken up with the objective of the present expedition.

When the first reports of apparitions had been radioed in to Aesop a check was made of the geodesic map of Saladin which was being built up in the computer decks. It revealed evidence of bed-rock reshaping having been carried out three thousand years earlier, in locations which corresponded closely with those of the sightings.

At that stage Aesop had withdrawn the survey modules, in keeping with the limitations of the Cartographical Service's charter, and a tachyonic transmission had been sent to the regional headquarters. As a result the cruiser *Admiral Carpenter*, which had been traversing that volume of space, arrived two days later and assumed control.

One of the first orders issued by Colonel Nietzel, commander of the ground forces, was that Aesop was to treat all information about Saladin as classified and to withhold it from civilian personnel. This should have meant that the *Sarafand*'s crewmen were completely in the dark about subsequent events, but there was some social contact between the two ships' complements, and Surgenor had heard the rumours.

Scanner satellites thrown into orbit by the *Admiral Carpenter* were reputed to have recorded thousands of partial materializations of buildings, strange vehicles, animals and heavily-robed figures right across the face of Saladin. It was also said that some of the buildings and figures had materialized into full solidity, but had vanished before any of the military vessel's fliers could reach them. It was as if another civilization existed on Saladin – one which had withdrawn beyond an incomprehensible barrier at the approach of strangers, and was determined to remain aloof.

Surgenor, who had not seen any of the apparitions, did not give much credence to the rumours, but he had seen the *Admiral Carpenter*'s fliers scream away across the desert at high supersonic speed, only to return empty-handed. And he knew that the cruiser's central computer was working on a round-the-clock basis on the task of correlating the vast amounts of data coming in from the network of scanner satellites.

He also knew that the grid co-ordinates Giyani had shown him corresponded to one of the ancient bedrock excavations which had been discovered in the initial survey ...

'How much further do you make it?' said Giyani, as the sun touched the distant range of hills on the western horizon.

Surgenor glanced at his mapscope, which was beginning to glow with the onset of darkness. 'Just under thirty kilometres.'

'Good. Our timing is exactly right.' Giyani let his hand fall on the butt of his sidearm.

'Going to shoot some spooks?' Surgenor said casually.

Giyani glanced down at his hand and then at Surgenor. 'Sorry. The orders are that I'm not allowed to discuss the operation with you. It's nothing personal, *Dave*, but if we had suitable ground transport of our own you wouldn't even be here.'

'But I am here, and I'm going to see what goes on.'

'That puts you ahead of the game, doesn't it?'

'I hadn't noticed.' Surgenor stared gloomily at the expanses of sand unfolding in the module's viewscreens, watching them turn from white to blood-red as the last traces of light sifted downwards out of the slant-rayed sky. In a few minutes there would be the typical Saladinian night scene of black-seeming desert and a clear sky so packed with stars that the normal order of things seemed to be reversed, that the land was dead and the sky above was the seat of life. He experienced an intense longing to be back on board the *Sarafand*, and travelling to far suns.

Lieutenant Kelvin leaned forward and spoke to Giyani. 'When can we expect to see something?'

'Any time now – assuming the computer prediction is accurate.' Giyani gazed impassively at Surgenor for a moment, obviously deciding whether to release information in his hearing, then shrugged. 'There is some geodesic evidence that bedrock reshaping was done in this area about a third of a million years ago, just around the time we think the Saladinians were in their city-building phase. The scanner satellites have glimpsed a city here seven times in the past ten days, but there is no guarantee – so I'm told – that the pattern of appearances the computer sees isn't purely coincidental, in which case we'll find nothing but desert.'

'What's so special about this particular site?' Kelvin said, echoing the question which had crossed Surgenor's mind.

'If the Saladinians can move freely *in time* – as some of our people think they can – then the quasi-materialization of buildings might be just a by-product of the natives themselves visiting the present. It sounds like a cooked up thing to me, but the Colonel was told to tell me that it's analogous to when you walk out of a heated building – you take some of the warm air with you into another environment. At each appearance of this city our scanners detected what seems to have been a woman standing on the southern fringe of the site.'

Giyani drummed on the armrest with his fingers. 'I'm also told that this woman was solid. As solid as any of us.'

Listening to the major's words, Surgenor felt the familiar cockpit of *Module Five* – in which he had spent so many hours of his life – become momentarily unfamiliar. Its dials and gauges were rendered meaningless for a brief period during which his mind was yielding to new concepts. He had been unwilling to admit his own fears that Man, perfector of a type of thinking which had given him mastery of the three spatial dimensions, had finally encountered a cooler, more judicious culture which had established its dominions in the long grey estuaries of time. But it appeared that other men were thinking along the same lines, reaching the same conclusions.

'Something up ahead, sir,' Kelvin said.

Giyani turned to face the front again and they all stared in silence at the forward viewscreen upon which the ghostly outlines of a cityscape were etching themselves from horizon to horizon. Regular patterns of light glowed where a few seconds earlier there had been nothing but sand and random stars.

The city's transparent rectangles were surprisingly Earth-like in design, except for one incongruity – the vertical rows of lights, which looked like windows, were not always superimposed on the silhouettes of the buildings. It was as if, Surgenor thought, the city was being seen not as it had existed at a single point in time, but with a temporal depth of focus extending over thousands of years during which the slow drift of continents had moved it several metres, thus producing a double image.

In spite of Giyani's facile explanation for what they were now seeing, or perhaps because of it, Surgenor began to feel chilled. He was beginning to appreciate the enormity of what the little expedition hoped to achieve.

'Reduce speed and go the rest of the way on the ground,' Giyani said. 'We want to travel quietly from here on in. Douse lights, too.'

Surgenor eased off the lift and cut the ground speed to fifty. At that rate, and with the absence of landmarks with which to judge speed, the survey module seemed to be at rest. The only sounds in the cabin were Kelvin's unsteady breathing and a series of faint clicks from McErlain's rifle as the sergeant adjusted various settings.

Giyani glanced over his shoulder at McErlain. 'How long is it since you served with the *Georgetown*, sergeant?'

'Eight years, sir.'

'Quite a long time.'

'Yes, sir.' McErlain sat quietly for a moment. 'I'm not going to shoot anybody unless ordered to, if that's what you're getting at. Sir.'

'Sergeant!' Kelvin's voice was scandalized. 'I'm putting you on report for ...'

'It's all right,' Giyani said easily. 'The sergeant and I understand each other.'

Surgenor was briefly distracted from the incredible view which lay ahead. He now knew why McErlain had been under discussion in the *Sarafand*'s mess. Ten or eleven years earlier the *Georgetown* had made first contact with an intelligent air-breathing species on a planet on the frontiers of the Bubble. And in a ghastly debacle, the details of which had never been officially released, had annihilated all the functional males in a single military action. The planet had since been sealed off from the Federation's normal commerce to allow its final generation of females and non-functional males to make their own way into oblivion in peace. The *Georgetown*'s commander had been court-martialled, but the 'incident' had passed

77

into the catalogue of self-indictments which humanity preserved in place of a racial conscience.

'Keep going at this speed till we reach the south side of the city,' Giyani ordered.

'We'll need lights.'

'We won't. Those buildings don't exist, except in a very attenuated form. Drive straight on.'

Surgenor allowed the module to continue on its original course and the insubstantial cityscape faded before him like fine mist. When he judged they were in the heart of the ancient site there was nothing to be seen but for an occasional suggestion of a streetlamp of curious trapezoid design, so faint that they might have been reflections of very clear glass.

'The buildings haven't dematerialized,' Kelvin said. 'Nobody ever got this close before.'

'Nobody had sufficiently processed the data before,' Giyani replied abstractedly, tracing the line of his black moustache with a fingertip. 'I have a feeling that the computer prognostication is going to check out right down to the last detail.'

'You mean ...'

'That's right, Lieutenant. To me it's almost a certainty that our Saladinian is a pregnant female.'

nine

The grid reference Surgenor had been given was so precise that he could have put the module on the designated spot with cross-hair accuracy, but Giyani told him to halt two hundred metres short. He opened the doors and waited until the three soldiers had stepped out on to the dark sand. The desert air was cold, the nightly temperature drop on Saladin being accentuated by the fact that the surface sand, by turning white during its exposure to sunlight, reflected away much of the day's heat instead of absorbing it.

'This should only take a few minutes,' Giyani said to Surgenor. 'We'll want to move off immediately we get back, so I want you to stay here and remain alert. Keep your motors turning and be ready to head north as soon as I give the word.'

'Don't worry, Major – I won't want to sit around here.'

Giyani put on goggle-like nightviewers and handed a pair to Surgenor. 'Put those on and keep watching us. If you see anything going seriously wrong, get out of here and then radio the ship.'

Surgenor put the viewers on and blinked as he saw Giyani's face etched with unnatural reddish light. 'Are you expecting trouble?'

'No – just being prepared.'

'Major, is it not true that there's a full-scale diplomatic mission on its way to this planet?'

'What of it, Surgenor?' Giyani's voice had lost its specious friendliness.

'Colonel Nietzel might want a feather in his cap – but other people might say he was improperly dressed.'

'The Colonel isn't exceeding his authority, driver – but you are.'

The three soldiers moved quietly away from the survey module and Surgenor looked beyond them for the first time. It was curiously difficult to focus his eyes – a sensation rather like peering through a badly adjusted tridi viewer – but he picked out an upright figure, so motionless that it might have been a spar of wood driven into the sand.

He felt a mixture of emotions – awe compounded with fear and respect. If all the theories were valid he was looking at a representative of the most formidable culture men had yet encountered in their blind thrusts across the galaxy, a race which breasted the river of time as easily as a starship crossed the graviton tides of space. Every instinct he had told him that such beings should be approached with reverence, and only after they had indicated their willingness to traffic in ideas, but it was obvious that Giyani had other ideas.

The major was prepared to use force against an entity which had the power to slip through his fingers like smoke. On the face of it, the action was ill-conceived and doomed to failure – and yet Giyani was an intelligent man. Surgenor frowned as he remembered the major's comment about the Saladinian being a pregnant female . . .

The alien figure moved suddenly, its grey shrouds swirling, as the three men drew near. Giyani advanced on it and for a few seconds it looked as though a conversation was being attempted, then the hooded figure turned away. One of the soldiers threw something and a hissing cloud of gas enveloped the retreating figure. It sagged to the ground and remained motionless.

The three soldiers lifted the inert alien and carried it towards the module. Surgenor engaged the drive and swung the vehicle closer to them, with its nose pointing north.

For a moment, during the slowing turn, the desert seemed to be alive with flickers of light and swooping, shrouded figures, but the illusion faded abruptly and by the time he had slid the module to a halt there was nothing visible but the three humans and their strange burden.

In a few seconds they were inside the vehicle. Surgenor twisted in his seat and looked at the unconscious alien on the floor. Even with the aid of the nightviewers he could barely discern a pale oval face in an aperture of the flowing robes. It *is* a female, he thought, then wondered how he knew.

'Get moving,' Giyani snapped. 'At top speed, mister.'

Surgenor selected air cushion suspension and engaged forward drive before the module had properly cleared the ground. It accelerated northwards in a snaking, waltzing surge of power, trailing a huge fantail of upflung sand.

Giyani relaxed into his seat with a sigh. 'That's the way to do it. Don't slow down until you see the ships.'

Surgenor became aware that he could smell the alien. The module's cabin was filled with a sweet musky odour, reminiscent of Concord grapes or some other fruit he had not tasted since his childhood. He wondered if it was the female's natural scent or an artificial perfume, then decided it was probably the former.

'How long will it take us to get back?' Giyani said.

'About an hour at this rate.' Surgenor increased the brightness of his control panel lights. 'Not that speed will help us any.'

'What does that mean, David?' Giyani's voice was throaty with excitement or satisfaction.

'If the Saladinians really can move about in time there's no point in trying to surprise them, or in trying to evade them, either. All they have to do is go back a few hours and stop you before you even started.'

'They didn't do it, did they?'

'No, but we couldn't hope to predict the way they will think or react in any given situation. Their minds are bound to be ...' Surgenor broke off as the alien on the floor gave a tremulous moan. At the same instant more ghostly flickers of light appeared and faded on the dark surface of the desert ahead, and it crossed his mind that the two events might be connected in some way which was beyond his understanding or previous experience.

'We should slow down, Major,' he said, making a fumbling effort to visualize time as a highway with hour-markers in place of milestones. 'At this speed we have a longish stopping distance, which means a longish stopping *time*, and that could make us easier targets.'

'Targets?'

'Easier to see. In time, I mean. It makes us more predictable ...'

'I've got an idea, David.' Giyani turned in his seat and grinned back at Kelvin as he spoke. 'Why don't you take a couple of minutes before dinner tonight and write us a tactical handbook? I'm sure that Colonel Nietzel would be grateful for any guidance you could give him.'

Surgenor shrugged. 'It was just a thought.'

'You could call it "Tactics For Temporal Confrontation".' Giyani was unwilling to forego his joke. 'By D. Surgenor, bus driver.'

'All right, Major,' Surgenor said resignedly, 'don't flog it to ...'

His voice was lost as, without warning, *Module Five* was drenched in blinding greenish light. *Sunlight*, he thought incredulously.

And then the massive vehicle was falling.

Images of lush green foliage whipped across the viewscreens as the module tilted, struck the ground on one side and bounded upwards again. There was a series of sharp reports as it mowed down a thicket of small trees, blanking out most of the viewscreens in the process as the sensors were wiped off the outer skin. Finally the vehicle slid to a halt in a tangle of ropy vegetation, and the thunderous sound of its progression gave way to a fretful hissing of gas escaping from a ruptured pipe. A few seconds later the shrill insistent bleeping of an alarm circuit announced that the cabin was becoming contaminated with radioactive matter.

Surgenor released himself from the clamps which had automatically sprung from the back of his seat at the first impact. He threw open the door nearest him, admitting a billow of hotly humid air of a kind which – his instincts told him immediately – the planet Saladin had not known in geological ages.

ten

They moved back along the rough path which *Module Five* had created until the polyrad dial on Surgenor's wrist showed they were at a safe distance from the radioactive spillage inside the vehicle.

Kelvin and McErlain set the shrouded alien woman down gently, making sure that her back was supported against the stump of a tree. Although they had carried her only a short distance their uniforms were pied with sweat. Surgenor felt his own clothing bind itself to his arms and thighs, but the physical discomfort was insignificant compared to the mental stress of dislocation. Night had become day, and in the same instant desert had become jungle. The hot yellow sun – the *impossible* sun – speared savagely into his eyes, blinding him, racking him with dismay.

'One of two things has happened,' Giyani said emotionlessly, sitting down on a tree trunk and massaging his ankle. 'We're in a different place at the same time – or we're in the same place at a different time.' He met Surgenor's gaze squarely. 'What do you say, David?'

'I say the first rule in that book on tactics by D. Surgenor, bus driver, will be "Drive slowly" – the way I told you earlier. We almost got ourselves ...'

'I know you say that, David. I admit you made a good point back there, or *then*, but what else do you say?'

'It looks as though we ran into the Saladinian equivalent of a landmine. I thought I saw something moving just before we hit.'

'A mine?' Kelvin said, looking around him with hurt eyes, and Surgenor realized for the first time that the lieutenant was barely out of his teens.

Giyani nodded. 'I'm inclined to agree. A time bomb, you might call it. We got ourselves a prisoner, and the Saladinians weren't prepared to stand for that. In similar circumstances we might have used a bomb which would have repositioned the target in space, but the natives here don't think the way we do ...'

'A surveyor is bound to have picked up some geology, David – how far back would you say we've been thrown?'

'I don't know all that much about geology, and the evolutionary timescales are bound to vary from planet to planet, but ...' Surgenor made a gesture which took in the surrounding walls of glossy green vegetation, the silent and humid air, and the riotous sun.

'For a climatic change of this magnitude you can probably talk in terms of millions of years. One, ten, fifty – take your pick.' He listened to his own words in fascination, marvelling at his body's ability to go on functioning with every appearance of normality in spite of what had happened.

'As far as that?' Giyani still sounded calm, but thoughtful now.

'Would it make any difference if I'd said only a thousand years? We've been eliminated, Major. There's no way back.' Surgenor tried to accept the fact as he spoke, but he knew the reaction would come later. Giyani nodded slowly, Kelvin lowered his face into cupped hands, and McErlain stood impassively staring at the hooded figure of the Saladinian woman. With one part of his mind Surgenor noted that the heavily-built sergeant was still holding the rifle, which apparently never left his hands.

'There might be a way back,' McErlain said, with an obstinate expression on his face. 'If we could get some information out of *her*.' He indicated the woman with his rifle.

'I doubt it, sergeant.' Giyani looked unimpressed.

'Well, they made bloody certain we didn't get her back to the ship. Risked killing her. Why was that?'

'I don't know, sergeant, but you can stop pointing that rifle at the prisoner – we can't afford any massacres here.'

'Sir?' McErlain's rough-hewn features were grim.

'What is it, sergeant?'

'I just wanted to tell you that the next time you make a crack about me and the *Georgetown*,' McErlain said in flat tones, 'you'll get the butt of this rifle down your throat.'

Giyani jumped to his feet, his brown eyes wide with shock. 'Do you know what I can do to you for that remark?'

'No, but I'm real interested, Major. Lay it on the line.' The sergeant was holding his rifle as casually as ever, but it had acquired significance.

'I can start by removing that weapon from you.'

'You think so?' McErlain smiled, showing uneven but exceptionally white teeth, and Surgenor suddenly became aware of him as a human being instead of as a cutout military figure. The two uniformed men faced each other in the jungle's sweltering silence. Watching the brilliantly lit tableau, Surgenor felt his attention being distracted by a curious irrelevancy. There was an incongruity somewhere. There was something strangely out of place, or lacking about the whole primeval scene . . .

The Saladinian woman whimpered faintly and sat upright with deliberate, painful movements. McErlain went towards her and with an abrupt movement threw the grey cowl back from her head.

Surgenor felt a vague sense of shame as he saw the alien face in bright, uncompromising light. The blurred glimpse he had caught in the darkness of the module's cabin had left him with an impression not of beauty – that hardly seemed possible – yet of some degree of compatibility with human standards of beauty. But here in the fierce sunlight there was no disguising the fact that her nose was a shapeless mound, that her eyes were much smaller than a human's, or that her black hair was so coarse that the individual strands gleamed separately like enamelled wire.

For all that, he thought, *there's no doubt that this is a woman*. He wondered if there could be a cosmic female principle which made itself obvious at first glance, even to an alien, then felt oddly uncomfortable as he realized he had thought of himself as the alien.

Further plaintive sounds came from the Saladinian's dry-lipped mouth as she turned her head from side to side, her plum-coloured eyes flicking over the four men and the background of jungle.

'Go ahead, sergeant,' Giyani said sardonically. 'Interrogate the prisoner and find out how to travel a million years into the future.'

Surgenor turned to him. 'Have we anything at all on the Saladinian language?'

'Not a word. In fact, we don't even know if they employ words – it might be one of those continuously inflected hums or buzzes that we've found on some planets.' He narrowed his eyes as the alien

84

woman got to her feet and stood swaying slightly, her pale skin glistening with oily secretions.

'She keeps looking back that way,' Lieutenant Kelvin said loudly, pointing down the avenue of shattered trees and uprooted vegetation in the direction from which the module had come. He ran a few paces along the trail with a boyish lope. 'Major! There's something back here. A tunnel or something.'

'Impossible,' Surgenor said instinctively, but he climbed up on a fallen trunk and shaded his eyes against the sun. At the far end of the trail he picked out a circular area of blackness. It looked like the mouth of a cave or tunnel, except that there was no visible background of hillside.

'I'm going to have a look.' Kelvin's tall spare figure bounded farther away from the group.

'Lieutenant!' Giyani spoke crisply, assuming command again after his inconclusive brush with McErlain. 'We'll go together.'

He looked directly at the Saladinian, then pointed down the trail. She appeared to understand at once and began walking, gathering the skirts of her robe exactly as an Earth woman would have done it. The sergeant fell in behind her with his rifle. Surgenor, walking beside McErlain, noted that the woman seemed to be moving with some difficulty, almost as if she were ill, but with a subtle difference . . .

'Major, sir,' he said, 'we don't need any security precautions here – so how did you know in advance that the prisoner would be a pregnant female?'

'It seemed likely from blow-ups of the satellite photographs. The natives are usually much slimmer and more mobile than this one.'

'I see.' Surgenor got a disturbing thought – at any minute they could be faced with the daunting task of having to deliver an alien child, with none of the customary facilities. 'So why did we have to go for one that was pregnant?'

'When I said they were less mobile I was using the word in the full context of this planet.' Giyani fell back beside Surgenor and offered him a cigarette, which he accepted gratefully in the absence of his pipe. 'The scanner records show that pregnant natives don't flit through time as easily as the others. They materialize solidly, fully into the present, and when they've done it they stay around longer.

It seems harder for them to vanish.'

'Why should that be?'

Giyani shrugged and blew out a plume of smoke. 'Who knows? If it's all done by mental control, as it seems to be, perhaps the presence of another mind right inside her own body ties the female down a bit. We'd never have caught this one otherwise.'

Surgenor stepped carefully around a newly sheared tree stump. 'That's the other thing I don't understand. If the Saladinians are so anxious to avoid contact, why did they let a vulnerable female into a sector of space-time occupied by us?'

'Maybe their control over time isn't as good as they'd like it to be, just the way our grip over normal space isn't perfect. Since we landed on Saladin some of our intellectual types on the ship have been claiming the natives have proved that the past, present and future are co-existent. All right – they may be if you look at them from the right angle – but supposing the present is still more important than the other two in some way.

'It might be like a wave crest which drags the females along with it when they're ready to give birth. Maybe the foetus is tied to the present because it hasn't learned the mental disciplines, or ...'

'What's the point in going over all this woolly theorizing?' Giyani demanded, checking his own expansiveness. 'It doesn't change anything or get us anywhere.'

Surgenor nodded thoughtfully, revising his assessment of Giyani. He had guessed the major was an intelligent man walking into danger with his eyes open, but he had been guilty – as he had also been with McErlain – of regarding him as just another military stereotype with a closed, inflexible mind. His talk with Giyani had been instructive in more ways than one.

At that moment Surgenor got a glimpse of what lay ahead of him on the rough jungle track and he stopped thinking about the major.

A night-black disc about three metres in diameter was floating in the air, its lower rim a short distance above the ground. Its edges were blurred, shimmering, and when Surgenor drew closer he saw that the blackness of the disc was relieved by the intense glitter of stars.

eleven

The draped figure of the Saladinian lurched forward two paces and stopped. McErlain moved in between her and the strange black disc and forced her to move away from it.

'Keep her there, sergeant.' Giyani's voice sounded almost contented. 'We may be back in time for breakfast, after all.'

'This is what she was looking for,' Lieutenant Kelvin said. 'I'll bet it's a kind of lifeline. That's our own time through there.'

Surgenor shaded his eyes and peered upwards into the disc. The stars within *did* look exactly like those he had last seen wheeling above the Saladinian desert in the 23rd century AD, although he had to admit that all stars looked pretty much alike. He shivered, then noticed that a gentle breeze was playing on his back. The air currents appeared to be moving in the direction of the enigmatic disc. He began to pick his way through the stand of undamaged vegetation which separated the end of the gouged-out trail from the circle of jet blackness.

'What are you doing, David?' Giyani said alertly.

'Just carrying out a little experiment.' Surgenor got closer to the disc, the lower edge of which was just above his head. He drew deeply on his cigarette and blew the smoke upwards. It travelled vertically for a short distance and was sucked into the blackness. He threw the remainder of the cigarette in after it. The white cylinder gleamed briefly in the sunlight, and did not complete its trajectory on the other side of the disc.

'Pressure differential,' he said, rejoining the group. 'The warm air is flowing through into that hole. Into the future, I guess.'

He, Giyani and Kelvin forced their way through the vegetation until they were on the other side of the disc, but from that standpoint in was nonexistent. There was nothing to see, except for McErlain impassively facing the Saladinian with his rifle lying in the crook of his arm. Giyani took a coin from his pocket and threw it in a twinkling arc which took it through the disc's estimated position. The coin fell to the ground near McErlain.

'It looks tempting,' Giyani said as they moved back round to their starting point, watching the blackness grow from a vertical line through an ellipse to a full circle. 'It would be comforting to think that we have only to jump through that hoop to arrive safely back in our own time – but how can we be sure?'

Kelvin clapped a hand to his forehead. 'But it's obvious, sir. Why else would it be there?'

'You're being emotional, Lieutenant. You're so anxious to get back to the ship that you're casting the Saladinians as benevolent opponents who clean you out at poker then give you your money back at the end of the game.'

'Sir?'

'Why should they hit us with a time bomb, and then rescue us? How do we know there isn't a thousand-metre drop on the other side of that hole?'

'They couldn't rescue their own female if that was the case.'

'Who says? After we had jumped through and killed ourselves they could re-focus it in some way and let the prisoner stroll through in safety.'

Kelvin's smooth face was clouded with doubt. 'That's pretty devious, sir. How about if we pushed the prisoner through first?'

'And perhaps have them close the thing up on us? I'm not trying to be devious, Lieutenant. We just can't afford a wrong assumption in this case.'

Giyani went to the silent woman, pointed at the disc and made an arcing movement with his hand. She stared at him for a moment, hissed faintly and duplicated his gesture. Her gaze returned to McErlain's face and the sergeant's eyes locked with hers as if they had entered some kind of rapport. Surgenor began to watch them.

'There you are, sir,' Kelvin said. 'We're supposed to go through.'

'Are you positive, Lieutenant? Can you guarantee me that when a Saladinian repeats a gesture it doesn't mean "negative" or "cancel"?'

Surgenor pulled his gaze away from the sergeant. 'We have to make *some* assumptions, Major. Let's throw something fairly heavy through the circle and find out if it makes a noise when it comes down on the other side.'

Giyani nodded. Surgenor went to the shallow crater caused by *Module Five*'s initial contact with the ground and picked up a football-sized rock. He brought it back and, using both hands, lobbed it up into the circle of darkness. Its disappearance was followed by complete silence.

'That doesn't prove anything,' Surgenor said, reneguing on his own experiment. 'Perhaps sound doesn't pass through the opening.'

'Sound is vibration,' Giyani said pedantically. 'Starlight is vibration, too, and we can see stars in there.'

'But . . .' Surgenor began to lose his temper. 'I'm prepared to take my chances, anyway.'

'I've got it,' Kelvin put in. 'We can get a downwards view.' Without waiting for permission from the major he swarmed up the silver bole of a tree and inched out on a horizontal bough which extended fairly close to the dark circle. When he was as close as he could get he stood up, balancing precariously by holding on to springy upper branches, and shaded his eyes.

'It's all right, sir,' he shouted. 'I can see the desert floor in there!'

'How far down?'

'Less than a metre. It's at a higher level than the ground here.'

'That's what caused the impact when we came through,' Surgenor said. 'We're lucky the level had altered so little in a few million years or so.'

Unexpectedly, Giyani smiled. 'Good work, Lieutenant. Come down from there and we'll build some kind of a ramp up to the lower edge.'

'Why bother?' Kelvin's voice was taut and there was a desperate grin on his face. 'I can make it from here.'

'*Lieutenant!* Come . . .' Giyani's voice faded away as Kelvin made an ungainly leap towards the circle. The lieutenant appeared to slip as he was jumping off, losing valuable height, but he tilted himself forward in the air as though diving into water. As his body was disappearing through the lower half of the circle one of his legs intersected the edge of the blackness, just at the ankle. A brown army boot fell into the vegetation below with an unpleasantly heavy thud. Even before he glimpsed the redness of blood, Surgenor knew that Kelvin's foot was still in the boot.

'The young fool,' Giyani said disgustedly. 'He's finally managed to finish himself.'

'Never mind that,' Surgenor shouted. 'Look at the circle!'

The black disc of night was shrinking.

Surgenor watched in arctic fascination as the circle contracted steadily, like the iris of an eye reacting to strong light, until its diameter was reduced to roughly two metres. Even when the inward movement had ceased he kept staring at the edge, reassuring himself that the portal to the future was not going to vanish completely.

'That's bad,' Giyani whispered. 'That's very bad, David.'

Surgenor nodded. 'It looks as though the power which keeps that hole open partially expends itself when something passes through. And if the shrinkage is proportional to the mass transmitted ... What diameter would you say it was before Kelvin went through?'

'About three metres.'

'And it's about two now – which means the area has been ... halved.'

The three men stared at each other as they performed the simple piece of mental arithmetic which made them mortal enemies. And slowly, instinctively, they began to move apart.

twelve

'I very much regret this,' Major Giyani said soberly, 'but there is no point in continuing the discussion. There can be no argument about who has to go through next.' The late afternoon sun, reflecting from the unbroken green of the jungle vegetation, made his face appear paler than normal.

'That means you, of course.' Surgenor looked down at his hands, which were cut in several places from the work of building a crude ramp up to the lower rim of the circle.

'Not *of course* – it simply happens that I am the only one here who has had a thorough briefing on the whole Saladinian situation. That fact, coupled with my special training, means that my report on this affair would be of greater value to Staff than one from either of you.'

'I question that,' Surgenor said. 'How do you know I haven't got an eidetic memory?'

'This could become childish, but how do you know *I* haven't got one?' Giyani's right hand descended, with seeming carelessness, on to the butt of his sidearm. 'Anyway – with hypno techniques available it isn't a question of what can be remembered, but of what one has taken the trouble to observe.'

'In that case,' McErlain put in, 'what have you observed about this jungle?'

'What do you mean, sergeant?' Giyani said impatiently.

'Simple question. There's something very unusual about this jungle we're in. A real hotshot observer like you is bound to have picked it up by this time – so what is it?' McErlain paused. 'Sir.'

Giyani's eyes flicked sideways. 'This is no time for parlour games.'

The sergeant's words had struck a chord in Surgenor's memory, reminding him that he too had sensed something out of place about their surroundings, something which made them different from any other jungle he had ever been in. 'Go on,' he said.

McErlain glanced around triumphantly, almost possessively, before he spoke. 'There aren't any flowers.'

'So what?' Giyani looked baffled.

'Flowers are designed to attract insects. That's the way most plants reproduce – through winged bugs getting pollen on their legs and bodies and spreading it around. All this stuff,' McErlain waved at the surrounding palisades of foliage, 'has been forced to reproduce some other way. Some other way which doesn't depend on . . .'

'Animal life!' Surgenor blurted the words out, wondering how he could have failed to complete the discovery earlier. This jungle, the ancient green world of Saladin, was *quiet*. No animals moved in its undergrowth, no birds sang, no insects throbbed in the still air. It was a world without any form of mobile life.

'Quite an interesting observation,' Giyani said coldly, 'but hardly relevant to the immediate problem.'

'That's what you think.' McErlain spoke with a savage intensity which caused Surgenor to look at him more closely. The big sergeant appeared to be standing at ease, but his eyes were locked on Giyani. He had positioned himself close to the silent Saladinian woman, closer than one might have expected under the circumstances. It was almost as if – the thought disturbed Surgenor – he and the alien woman had begun to share a bond.

Surgenor turned his attention to the ramp they had built with trees felled by the module. The base of it was only a few paces away

91

from him, and he could have sprinted up it to reach the portal in as little as two seconds – but he was certain that the sergeant could burn him down in a fraction of that time. His main hope seemed to lie in Giyani and McErlain becoming so intent on their own conflict that they would forget to keep an eye on him. He edged closer to the ramp and tried to think of a way to steer the two soldiers into a direct confrontation.

'Major,' he said casually, 'you say your principal concern is with the overall situation? With serving Earth's interests in the best way possible?'

'That's correct.'

'Well, has it occurred to you that the Saladinians didn't set up that tunnel, lifeline, or whatever it is, for our benefit? Their sole concern was probably with rescuing the prisoner.'

'What of it?'

'In that case, you have a chance to make a really important gesture of goodwill. One which might make the Saladinians much more co-operative with our forces. If we sent the prisoner through to her own time . . .'

Giyani undid the retaining strap of his holster with a single rapid movement. 'Don't try to be clever with me, David. And move away from that ramp.'

Surgenor experienced an upsurge of fear, but did not move. 'How about it, Major. The Saladinian mind is so alien to us that we've no idea what that woman over there is thinking. We can't exchange a single thought or word with her or her people, but there'd be no mistaking *our* intentions if we sent her through the circle.' He put his foot on the base of the ramp.

'*Get back!*' Giyani gripped his sidearm and began to draw it clear of the holster.

McErlain's rifle clicked faintly. 'Take your hand away from the pistol,' he said quietly.

Giyani froze. 'Don't be a fool, sergeant. Don't you see what he's doing?'

'Just don't try to pull that pistol.'

'Who do you think you are?' Giyani's face darkened with barely suppressed fury. 'This isn't the . . .'

'Go on,' McErlain prompted with spurious pleasantness. 'Tell me

92

I'm not with the *Georgetown* any more. Let's have a few more genocide jokes – you like those, Major.'

'I wasn't . . .'

'You were! That's all I've had from you for the last year, Major.'

'I'm sorry.'

'Don't be – it was all true, you see.' McErlain's gaze travelled slowly from Giyani to the enigmatic figure of the Saladinian, and back again. 'I was one of the trigger men in that party. We didn't know anything about the way-out reproductive set-up the natives had. We didn't know that the handful of males had to preserve their honour and the honour of their race by making a ritual attack. All we saw was a bunch of shaggy centaurs coming at us with spears. So we burned 'em down.'

Surgenor shifted his weight in preparation for a dash up the single tree trunk which was the spine of the ramp.

'They kept coming at us,' McErlain continued, his eyes dull with pain. 'So we kept on burning 'em down – and that's all there was to it. We didn't find out till afterwards that we had wiped out all the functional males, or that they wouldn't have done us any harm anyway.'

Giyani spread out his hands. 'I'm sorry, McErlain. I didn't know how it was, but we've got to talk about the situation right here, right *now*.'

'But that's what I am talking about, Major. Didn't you know?' McErlain looked puzzled. 'I thought you'd have known that.'

Giyani took a deep breath, walked towards the sergeant and when he spoke his voice was unwavering. 'You're a thirty-year old man, McErlain. You and I know what that means to you. Now, listen to me carefully – I am ordering you to hand me that rifle.'

'You're *ordering* me?'

'I'm ordering you, sergeant.'

'By what authority?'

'You already know that, sergeant. I'm an officer in the armed forces of the planet you and I were born on.'

'An officer!' McErlain's expression of bafflement grew more pro-nounced. 'But you don't understand. Not anything . . . When did you become an officer in the armed forces of the planet you and I were born on?'

Giyani sighed, but decided to humour the sergeant. 'On the tenth of June, 2276.'

'And because you're an officer you're entitled to give me orders?'

'You're a thirty-year man, McErlain.'

'Tell me this . . . sir. Would you have been entitled to give me orders on the *ninth* of June, 2276?'

'Of course not,' Giyani said soothingly. He extended his hand and grasped the muzzle of the rifle.

McErlain did not relax his grip. 'What date is it now?'

'How can we tell?'

'Let me put it another way – is this later than the tenth of June, 2276? Or earlier?'

Giyani showed the first signs of strain. 'Don't be ridiculous, sergeant. In a situation like this, subjective time is what counts.'

'That's a new one on me,' McErlain commented. 'Is it part of Regulations, or did you get it from the book which is going to be written by our friend over there who thinks I can't see him edging on to the ramp?'

Surgenor took his foot off the silvery trunk and waited, with a growing conviction that an inexplicable and dangerous new element had been added to the situation. The Saladinian had drawn the hood back over her head, but her eyes seemed to be fixed on McErlain. Surgenor could almost believe that she understood what the sergeant was saying.

'It's like that is it?' Giyani shrugged, walked away from McErlain and leaned against the base of a large yellow-leaved tree. He turned his attention to Surgenor. 'Is it just my imagination, David, or is that circle still shrinking a little?'

Surgenor inspected the black disc with its incongruous sprinkling of stars, and his sense of urgency was intensified. The circle did appear to be fractionally smaller.

'It might be due to the air blowing through there,' he said. 'Humid air has a lot of mass . . .'

He stopped speaking as Giyani quickly moved behind the tree against which he had been leaning. From Surgenor's vantage point he was able to see the major clawing out his sidearm. He threw himself into the lee of the ramp for protection, knowing in his heart that it was totally inadequate, and in the same instant McErlain's rifle emitted a blaze of man-made lightning. The rifle must have been set at maximum power, because the ultralaser ray sliced explosively clear through the thickness of the tree trunk – and then through Giyani's chest. He went down in a welter of blood and fire. The tree rocked for a few seconds, grinding the ashes in the blackened cross-section, and tilted away to sprawl noisily downwards through other trees.

Belatedly acknowledging that the ramp offered him no shelter, Surgenor got to his feet and faced McErlain. 'My turn now?'

The sergeant nodded.

'You'd better dive through that hole before it disappears,' he said.

'But ...' Surgenor stared at the ill-matched couple – Sergeant McErlain and the small grey figure of the Saladinian woman – and his mind began to teem with conjecture. 'Aren't you going?' he said, scarcely aware of the inanity.

'I have things to do.'

'I don't understand.'

'Do me a favour,' McErlain said. 'Tell them I put my record straight. I helped kill a planet once – now I'm helping to bring another one to life.'

'I still don't understand.'

McErlain glanced at the nameless alien woman. 'She's going to have a child soon, perhaps more than one. They'd never survive without my help. Food can't be all that plentiful.'

Surgenor walked up the ramp and stood beside the black circle. 'Suppose there isn't any food? How do you know any of you will survive?'

'We must,' McErlain said simply. 'Where do you think the people of this planet came from?'

'They could have come from anywhere. The chances that the Saladinian race originated here, at this point, are so small that ... Surgenor broke off, guiltily, as he saw the desperate need in McErlain's eyes.

He took one final look at the sergeant and his enigmatic companion, then dived cleanly through the black circle. There was a moment of fear as he fell into the darkness, then he rolled over on cold sand and sat up, shivering. The familiar stars of the Saladinian night sky shone overhead, but his attention was taken up by the circle from which he had emerged.

In this age it was a disc of greeenish light – looking from night into day – hovering above the desert floor. He watched as it shrank unsteadily to the size of a sun-blazing golden plate, to an eye-searing diamond. Air whistled through the aperture with a plaintively ascending note as it dwindled to a star and finally vanished.

When his eyes readjusted to the darkness he picked out the shape of Lieutenant Kelvin lying on the sand a short distance away. The blob of spray-on tissue-weld at his ankle was visible as a whitish blur.

'Do you need any help?' Surgenor asked.

'I've already put in a call,' Kelvin said faintly, without moving. 'They should be here soon. Where are the others?'

'Back there.' One part of his mind told Surgenor that McErlain and the Saladinian woman had been dead for millions of years, but another now understood they were still alive, because the past and the present and the future are as one. 'They can't make it.'

'That means . . . they've been dead for a long time.'

'You could say that.'

'Oh, Christ,' Kelvin whispered. 'What a stupid, pointless way to go. It's as if they'd never lived.'

'Not quite,' Surgenor said. It had just occurred to him that Sergeant McErlain's wish to help seed a world with new life might have been granted – literally. He did not know enough biology to let him be sure, but it seemed possible that – given, say, a hundred million years – the teeming organisms of a human body could thrive and spread right through a receptive environment, and then begin to evolve. After all, Saladin *had* produced an intelligent life form . . .

The scope of the speculation was too great for Surgenor in his shocked condition, but in another mental level he had an illogical flicker of hope that, somehow, the Saladinians would learn what McErlain had done for a member of their race. If that happened, they might just have the beginnings of the basis for a working relationship.

Kelvin sighed tiredly in the darkness. 'It's time we got off this planet anyway.'

Surgenor turned his gaze towards the sky. He could imagine himself back on board the *Sarafand* – travelling far and fast – but the after-image of the bright circle persisted in his vision for a long, long time, like an insubstantial sun.

*

McErlain stirred feebly in the dimness of the cave. He tried to call out, but the congestion in his lungs had grown so great that he produced only a faint, dry rattle. The small grey figure at the mouth of the cave did not move, but continued to stare patiently outwards at the rain-soaked banks of foliage. There was no way, even after all the years, of knowing if she heard him or not. He lay back and, as the fever intensified its hold, tried to reconcile himself to dying.

Summing it all up – he had been fortunate. The Saladinian woman had remained as uncommunicative as only an alien member of an alien race could do, but she had stayed with him, accepted his aid. He could swear he had seen something like gratitude in her eyes when he had helped her through the difficult period of the birth and her subsequent illness. That had been good for him.

Then there had been the times when he in turn lay ill; poisoned as a result of trying the wrong fruit or plants or seeds in his quest to find food suitable for her and the children. At those times, he fancied, she had never been far from his side.

Most gratifying of all was the fact that the Saladinian women and her kind were very fertile. The offspring of that first quadruple birth were young adults now, and had produced many more children. As he had watched them multiply, the cancer of guilt which had been devouring him since the Georgetown incident had ceased to dominate his life. It was still there, of course, but he had learned to forget it for hours on end.

If only he had been able to teach the children his own language, to drive one idea through the logic-structure barrier, things would have been better – but there was a limit to what a man could ask. He was a thirty-year man, McErlain decided as the conscious world tilted ponderously away from him, and it was enough that he had been given the chance to put his record straight . . .

Late that evening, as the sun's light was fleeing through the trees, the Family gathered around the bed on which McErlain's body lay. They stood in silence while the Mother laid one hand on the dewed, icy brow.

This being is dead, she told them silently. And now that our debt to him is paid, and his need for us has ended, we shall travel to the great home-time of our own people.

The children and adults joined hands. And the Family vanished.

thirteen

Surgenor was not a superstitious man, nor did he believe in luck – good or bad – but his years in the Cartographical Service had convinced him of the reality of what he called jackpot trips. These were missions on which the law of averages caught up with the *Sarafand* and its crew members. On a jackpot trip, blind chance – like a worker who has gone to sleep on the job and is belatedly trying to make up a quota – would cram all the incidents and mishaps which had been notably absent from a dozen previous sorties.

As defined by Surgenor, a jackpot trip could not be predicted in advance, but during the preparations for Survey 837/LM/4002a his instincts were curiously aroused.

The first trigger stimulus was the discovery that part of Aesop's memory, in a section of the astrogation data bank, had unaccountably decayed and needed to be replaced. A team of specialists from a newly registered contractor, Starfinders Incorporated, carried out the necessary substitutions and tests in only two days. The Service's own maintenance organization would have taken three times as long to perform an operation of similar scope, and Surgenor, who distrusted commercially motivated celerity in matters which concerned his own wellbeing, made his views known throughout the sector transit station.

'All it proves is that our maintenance people spend a lot of time playing cards,' Marc Lamereux assured him. 'It's the same with any big Government outfit – contractors always work faster because they have to be more efficient to show a profit.'

'I still don't like it.' Surgenor traced a design on the foggy prism of his lager glass and stared bleakly along the swimming pool where several men were playing ball. He had been living at the transit hotel on Delos for ten days and, as usual, was becoming restless.

'There was nothing to the job anyway,' Lamereux said with a peaceful expression on his dark countenance. 'Pull out a few equipment trays and shove in replacements. Two hours should be enough, let alone two days.'

'Listen to the intrepid astronaut,' Surgenor gibed, taking refuge in childishness. 'I seem to remember that you're the character who once signed a complaint about the texture of some beefburgers.'

'It was a knitted steak – and I could easily have choked to death that time.' Lamereux scowled, but only momentarily. 'Anyway, I've made up my mind to stop fretting about crew safety.'

'You've got religion.'

'No – my transfer.' Lamereux produced a printed green slip from his pocket. 'I've hooked that public relations job I've been trying for back on Earth. Shipping home tomorrow.'

'Congratulations.' Surgenor suddenly realized that ever since Lamereux had joined him at the pool ten minutes earlier he had been trying to engineer a suitably dramatic opening for his announcement. 'Hey, Marc! That's great! I hate to see you go after all our time together, but I know you're ready for a change.'

'Thanks, Dave.' Lamereux sipped his own lager. 'Five years, it's been. Five years on the edge of the Bubble. It's been a long time – but that's what helped me get the job.'

Five years is a long time in this job, Surgenor thought. *And I've been riding on the edge of the Bubble for almost twenty years.* The continued expansion of the spherical volume of space which men had explored and charted was placing an ever-increasing strain on the Cartographical Service's resources. That was why the survey missions were getting longer, and why men like him – who lacked the sense to retire – were being allowed to grow old in harness. It was also why the big ships were being kept in service long past their designed lifetimes. The trouble was that plug-in components were available for the ships, but not for their crews, and that he – Dave Surgenor – was bound to be wearing out and becoming obsolete every bit as fast as Captain Aesop.

'. . . some realism into the recruiting campaigns,' Lamereux was saying. 'It won't matter about pulling in less bodies if we can pare down the drop-out rate.'

'That's right – you make sure you tell 'em what's what when you get back there.' Surgenor decided to try elevating his spirits. 'I take it, young Marc, that you'll be throwing a party tonight.'

Lamereux nodded. 'It's all arranged. Old Beresford says we can have the roof garden bar all to ourselves.'

'He must be in a good mood, for once.' Surgenor frowned, remembering the sector administrator's lack of co-operation on similar occasions in the past. 'Has he finally won a prize for his crochet work?'

Lamereux looked maliciously amused. 'He thinks it'll be a good opportunity for you and the others to meet Christine.'

'Christine?'

'Christine Holmes. My replacement in *Module One*.'

'A woman?'

'With a name like Christine, that's a fairly safe bet. Anyway, what of it? We've had women crew members before this.'

'I know, but ...' Surgenor left the sentence unfinished, not wanting to give extra substance to his feelings by putting them into words. It was rare to find a woman among the Cartographical Service field crews. This was partly because of the physical demands – every crew member had, for example, to be able to change a survey module's wheels under any conditions – but Surgenor suspected the principal reason for their scarcity was that they saw no point in the work. He knew that a great majority of the planet maps he helped to construct would never be put to any practical use; but at the same time he understood that the maps had to be made, that the information had to be gathered and banked – even though he found it difficult to say exactly why. Most women, Surgenor believed, had little patience with this vague allegiance to the scientific ethos, and when working with them found himself tending towards a disastrous uncertainty about his whole way of life.

On this morning, however, his main concern was with the way in which random factors affecting Survey 837/LM/4002a had begun to combine. There had been no trouble with Aesop's memory of how to steer the ship through the gravitation currents of beta-space; the too-quick, too-effortless correction of the fault; the unexpected departure of Marc Lamereux; and now the discovery that Marc's place would be taken by a woman.

Surgenor was doing his best to be clear-headed and rational, but no amount of effort could purge his mind of the notion that he was about to begin the jackpot trip to end all jackpot trips.

The farewell party for Marc Lamereux started early and finished late, but in spite of consuming a large amount of alcohol Surgenor failed to get properly into the swing of it. He had made the tactical blunder of allowing himself to get high during the lunchtime drinks session by the pool, then had slept in the afternoon, with the result that the rest of the day was pretty much of a let-down as far as intoxication was concerned.

'It's like *post-coital triste*, except that it goes on and on,' he complained to Al Gillespie as they sat together at the bar. 'It must be a lesser-known law of nature – you can only get high once a day.'

Gillespie shook his head in disagreement. 'That's not a lesser-known law, Dave – it's one of the basic rules of boozing. When you start early in the day you've got to keep going.'

'Too late now.' Surgenor swallowed some neat whisky, which tasted warm and flat, and glanced about the discreetly lit glass-walled room in which the bar was situated. Beyond the exotic foliage of the roof garden the lights of the city curved to the horizon around a bay in which a hundred pleasure craft trailed luminous chevrons of disturbed water. Even the waves, exciting noctilucent marine creatures with their passage, seemed to be made of cool green fire, creating the impression that the sea had come to life while the land slept in darkness. And far above the canopies of artificial radiance a few first-magnitude stars shone patiently, waiting.

Surgenor, shut off from the boisterous merriment of his comrades, felt an unmanning pang of loneliness. Delos was a beautiful and hospitable world, but it was not his home; the men he called his friends, with whom he spent all his waking moments, were not really his friends. It was true that they treated him with amiable toleration and respect, but no other attitude was viable in the close confines of the ship, and were he to retire his replacement would be given exactly the same consideration.

Wilful strangers, he thought, recalling an old fragment of verse which for decades had served him as a personal creed. As used by the poet, the phrase had described men who chose never to remain long enough in any one place to become familiar with it, but it was being borne home to Surgenor that the survey crews – incomplete, flawed humans all – treated personal relationships in the same way. He, himself, was a prime example. He had chosen to live as a wilful stranger in a ship of strangers, and although he had known Marc Lamereux for five years neither man was any more than superficially perturbed at the thought of parting. And what greater indictment of his life-style could there be?

Looking back over his years with the *Sarafand*, Surgenor could

101

recall a succession of men who had joined the ship, stayed around for greater or lesser periods of time, and then had gone. Some of the faces in that dwindling temporal perspective were blurred; others stood out clearly for no particular reason. Clifford Pollen, whose sketchily researched book had finally seen print, was now a successful journalist with a colonial news agency. Young Bernie Hilliard had managed to buy himself out before his two-year stint had ended and had gone into junior school teaching on Earth. There had been dozens of others, all individual and yet with one thing in common – Surgenor had been mildly contemptuous of their lack of staying power. Now it appeared that what he had seen as failings on their parts could have been virtues. Did they represent valuable lessons about life which he had stubbornly failed to absorb?

An explosion of laughter followed by an outbreak of horseplay in another part of the room disturbed Surgenor's thoughts without altering his mood. He traded his stale drink for a fresh one and moved away from the bar to a quieter corner. The party had swollen to about fifty, the crew of the *Sarafand* having been joined by men from other ships and a sprinkling of transit station personnel. A number of girls were present, each of them enjoying the attentions of at least three young men, and it dawned on Surgenor that it would be good, so *very good*, to be able to talk to a woman on this night of sad revelation.

Unfortunately, attractive though the idea was, there was little he could do about putting it into practice. He was not going to jostle with young lusties in the hope of getting near a girl, who in any case was likely to see him as a father figure, nor was he going to leave the party to prowl in the city. It appeared there was nothing for it but to defy Gillespie's so-called basic law of boozing and try to get into the same alcoholic orbit as some of his colleagues. He swallowed a large portion of his drink and was moving closer to the group at the piano when a door opened and the stooped figure of Harold Beresford, the sector administrator, came into the bar. Accompanying him was a tall, slim woman with cropped dark hair and wearing a one-piece suit.

Surgenor stared jealously at the couple, wondering how the fussy and cantankerous executive, famous among the survey crews for his interest in needlework, had managed to show more foresight than himself by bringing a female companion to the party. The injustice he imagined in the situation was deepening Surgenor's gloom when he noticed a star cluster brooch on the woman's collar, and it came to him that in all probability she was Lamereux's replacement. Wondering if fate had decided to make special provision for him, Surgenor went straight to Beresford and shook his hand.

'David Surgenor, isn't it?' Beresford said, peering up into Surgenor's face. 'Good! You're just the man to show Christine around. Meet David Surgenor, Christine.'

'Call me Chris,' the woman said, grinning easily. Her handshake was firmer than Beresford's had been and Surgenor was aware of callouses at the base of her fingers.

'I was hoping to be able to stay for an hour myself, give our friend Lamereux a good send-off and all that, but I find I have to finish a report tonight.' Beresford smiled a nervous apology, excused himself and hurried out.

'My God, did you ever *see* such an old woman?' Christine said, nodding in the direction of the door. She was older than Surgenor had first thought, in her mid or late thirties, and was lean rather than slim, as though her body had been honed down by years of hard work.

'You'll soon get used to him,' Surgenor said, his romantic fantasies fading.

'I won't have to.' She gave Surgenor an appraising glance from deep-set, dark-shadowed eyes. 'I think he had reasons of his own for bringing me here tonight, but he hasn't got them any more.'

'You managed to turn him off?'

Christine nodded. 'I managed to scare the shit out of him.'

'That would do it,' Surgenor said. 'That would turn him off, all right.'

'You're damn right.' Christine craned her neck to look at the bar. 'What's a girl got to do to get a drink around here?'

Surgenor gave an admiring chuckle. 'Just name it. What would you like?'

'Straight Bourbon, and make it a tall one – it looks like I'm way behind everybody else.'

'Okay.' Surgenor fetched a drink to the required specification. By the time he had returned with it Christine had already joined the group at the piano and was harmonizing as though she had been with the *Sarafand* crew for years instead of minutes. She nodded a curt thanks to him as she took the glass, then turned back to the singers.

Surgenor went back to his original seat and got to work on his own drink, telling himself he was glad there was no chance of a jackpot trip being further complicated by undue femininity on the part of the new crew member.

fourteen

Surgenor came out through the main entrance of the Service hostel, filled his lungs with dew-cleansed morning air, and looked around for the shuttle which would carry him out to the Bay City terminal.

The silver-and-blue vehicle was waiting in the reserved section at the front of the parking area, its driver giving preliminary glances at his wristwatch. Surgenor walked across to it, slung the cases which contained all his personal possessions into the luggage bay, and climbed on board. The shuttle was three-quarters filled with departing surveyors and base personnel going out to begin a day's work at the field, and he nodded to familiar faces here and there as he made his way to an empty place. His own ship was not due to lift off until early in the afternoon, and he was mildly surprised therefore to see Christine Holmes watching him from the bench seat at the rear.

'On the road early,' he commented, sitting down beside her.

'I'm new to the job – this is only my second trip,' she said. 'What's your excuse?'

'I've been on Delos before.'

'So you're bored with it.' Christine examined him with undisguised curiosity. 'I hear you've been on survey work for twenty years.'

'Almost.'

'How many worlds have you covered?'

'A fair amount, I suppose – I'm not sure how many.' Surgenor wondered briefly why he was lying on this point – he knew precisely the number of planets he had traversed. 'Does it matter?'

'Not to me, it doesn't. But if you're bored after a couple of weeks' stopover on Delos, what's it going to be like when they put you out to grass?'

'Let me worry about that,' Surgenor said stiffly, annoyed at the forthrightness of the question. There was no rank structure on survey ships – an indication of the essentially casual nature of the work – but he felt that a raw novice could have chosen to show respect for his experience. Or was it that the question had touched a nerve, reminding him of his growing ambivalence towards the Service? How was he going to reconcile the life of a star gypsy with his need for stable and permanent relationships? What was to be his ultimate fate if it turned out that, literally, he was unable to stop travelling?

'Anyway,' he said, diverting his thoughts, 'what decided you to sign on?'

'Why? Don't tell me you're one of those dinosaurs who thinks a competent woman is some kind of freak.'

'Did I say that?'

'You didn't have to.'

'As a matter of fact, it's not your sex – it's your age,' Surgenor replied, losing his temper. 'You're about twice as old as most new starts.'

'I see.' Christine nodded, seemingly unoffended by his rudeness. 'Well, that's a fair question. I guess you could say I'm looking for a new career – something to take me out of myself, as they say. I had a husband once, and a son. And they both died. I wanted to get away from Earth, and I've got mechanical aptitudes, so I took a surveyor's course ... and here I am.'

'I'm sorry if I ...'

'It's all right, she said brightly. 'It was a long time ago – and they say everybody has to die sometime.'

Surgenor nodded a glum assent, wishing he had confined himself to remarks about the weather or, better still, had chosen a different seat. 'All the same, I'm sorry about ... about what I ...'

'That bitchy crack about my age? Forget it. Anyway, you're no spring chicken yourself, are you?'

'Too right,' Surgenor said, relieved at the return to undemanding banter. A few seconds later the shuttle's doors closed and the vehicle began its journey to the space terminal. The slanting rays of the sun, changing direction at each corner, threw a spotlight on Christine's strong-jawed face, emphasizing the pallor of her complexion. She smoked cigarettes almost continuously throughout the trip, occasionally getting ash on her own uniform and brushing it off on to

Surgenor's. He considered drawing her attention to the multitude of NO SMOKING signs in the shuttle, but a moment's reflection about the possible consequences persuaded him to remain silent. It was with a disproportionate sense of relief that he saw the terminal's perimeter fence begin to blur past the windows, followed by clusters of peripheral buildings and glimpses of the metal pyramids of the spacecraft themselves.

He unshipped his case and walked with Christine to the Service operations block where they went through signing-in procedures and the pre-flight medical checks. There were still three hours to go before the *Sarafand* crew's final muster. Surgenor hoped that Christine would stay in the crew lounge, but she opted to walk out to their ship with him. It was basically an eighty-metres-tall cylinder tapering to a point at the top, and with four triangular fairings on the lower third which made it into a slim pyramid. When Surgenor got closer he saw that considerable refurbishing had been done on the *Sarafand*. Most noticeable were the new rows of sacrificial anodes, the blocks of pure metal which acted as centres for electrical and chemical interactions between the ship and alien atmospheres, thus minimizing erosion of the entire hull. Unfortunately, the freshness of the anodes drew attention to the scarred dinginess of the surrounding metal.

'Is this it?' Christine said, as soon as their destination became obvious. 'Is it really and truly a Mark Six?'

'That's the mark that put our flag on three-quarters of the planets in the Bubble.'

'But is it still safe to fly in?'

Surgenor reached the entrance ramp first and started up it. 'If you've got any doubts,' he said, without looking back, 'this is the time to pack in the job. They don't really like crewmen funking out, but if anybody is going to funk out they prefer them to funk out at base, and not to funk out in the middle of a trip.'

Christine was close behind him when he reached the cavernous shade of the hangar deck, and she caught his arm. 'What's all this stuff about funking out, big man?'

'Did I cause offence?' Surgenor looked politely apologetic. 'I'm sorry. It was just that you seemed a little nervous down there.'

Christine stared at him with narrowed eyes which were almost on a level with his own. 'I get it. You identify with this beat-up old scow

– you actually *identify* with it. Boy, you really are in a mess!' She brushed past him before he could reply and marched towards the metal stair which led to the upper decks.

Surgenor gaped at her departing figure, outraged, then looked all around as though seeking a witness to the wrong which had been done him. The six survey modules crouched in their stalls gazed back at him with cyclopean headlights, noncommittal, uninvolved.

The take-off from Delos, in contrast to what was to follow, was a routine affair.

The *Sarafand* floated clear of the ground and rose steadily to a height of fifty metres, at which point – in compliance with inter-stellar quarantine regulations – she paused and electrostatically cleansed herself of the dust, pebbles and spacefield litter which were swirling within her counter-gravity field. There followed a one-gravity ascent to one hundred kilometres, and a second electrostatic purge which dispersed the last traces of captured atmosphere into the void. The ship was now set to make the first tentative beta-space jump, a short one which would take her clear of the gravitational complexities of the local sun and planetary system.

Surgenor knew that Aesop, using a part of his 'mind' which was inaccessible to the understanding of the crew members, was testing his environment, surveying the invisible slopes of space, making ready to perform geometric miracles. From his seat in the observation room, Surgenor stared down at the curving blue-white expanses of Delos and waited for the planet to vanish. As ever, in spite of all the years, he felt a slow build-up of excitement and his heart began a measured pounding.

He glanced along the row of swivel seats, taking stock of the company in which he was once again to leap into the unknown. Of the eleven other people present, only four – Victor Voysey, Sig Carlen, Mike Targett and Al Gillespie – were long-term veterans with the *Sarafand*. Some of the remainder had picked up limited experience on other ships before transferring to the *Sarafand*, and the rest, as was the case with Christine Holmes, were still in the novice stage.

Officially speaking, lack of service time or an abundance of it was of little importance – a newcomer to the job received virtually the same pay as an old hand – but Surgenor persisted in believing that

107

experience was valuable, and he would have preferred a higher proportion of veterans in the crew. It occurred to him as he waited that he was becoming morbidly conscious of risk factors – something which had not bothered him unduly in the old days. Was that why he had, so uncharacteristically, lost his temper with Christine Holmes?

A frisson of excitement rippled through the room as the curving bright solidity of the planet Delos flicked out of existence, causing a sudden drop in the light intensity. In its place a fiercely concentrated point of brilliance stood out against the background of stars. Surgenor knew he had travelled upwards of half a light-year in the instant of change, and that Aesop – immune to fear, untouched by wonder – was calmly preparing for the next leap, a huge one this time which would carry the *Sarafand* deep into unknown space. It was heading outwards from the plane of the Milky Way, its destination a loose grouping of five suns which burned like look-out fires on the edge of intergalactic space.

Even on Delos, Surgenor had been accutely aware of the sparseness of stars in that quarter of the night sky which lay to the galactic north – now the realization loomed large in his mind that, on the completion of the next beta-space jump, there would be *nothing* between him and the great void. The observation room had two hemispherical viewing screens, and while one of them overflowed with the profuse suns of the galaxy which had almost been left behind, the other would be empty except for the dim, blurry specks of distant island universes.

The Bubble is getting too big, Surgenor mused uneasily. It was true that the sphere of man's activity only extended through the thickness of the galactic wheel – and that most of its diameter, with all the multitudinous star systems of the hub – lay beyond his domain, but a boundary had been reached just the same. It was a reminder that the galaxy was finite. And that jaunty, querulous, presumptuous *homo sapiens* had a taste for the infinite . . .

'Hey, Dave!' Victor Voysey leaned across from the next chair and spoke in a whisper. 'I've just had a dust-up with Marc's replacement. I thought somebody said she was a woman.'

'She's had a rough time,' Surgenor said, glancing along the row. In profile Christine's shadow-eyed face looked almost haggard.

108

'That's as may be, but ... *Christ* ... I only told her nobody's allowed to smoke in the clean air rooms.'

Surgenor repressed a smile. 'Look out, infinity – some of us are coming to flick ash on you.'

'You feeling all right Dave?'

'Some day, Victor, maybe you'll learn not to rush in where ...' Surgenor gripped the arms of his chair as, within two seconds, the brilliant nucleus of the far-off sun of Delos snapped out of being, was replaced by an all-enveloping blackness in which a few misty blurs of light hovered like fireflies, then was replaced yet again by a different pattern of misty specks. Finally a wild extravagance of star fields – glittering and crowded, filling both hemispheres of vision – came blazing into existence.

Surgenor's heart seemed to stop beating altogether as it became obvious that something had gone wrong with the beta-space jump. It was totally unknown for a ship to make three transitions in rapid succession; and it was apparent that their present location, where ever it might be was not on the brink of starless deeps.

'Dave?' Voysey kept his voice low. 'Have we been on a joyride?'

'Joyride?' The inappropriateness of the word dragged at Surgenor's lips. 'I hope I'm wrong, but I got the impression that ... just for a second or so ... we were *outside*.'

'But Aesop wouldn't go out. It says in all the books that the graviton flux is too strong out there for a ship to have any kind of control. I mean, if we went out we wouldn't be able to ...'

'Let's discuss it later,' Surgenor said, inclining his head towards the other crew members. 'If something has gone wrong in Aesop's astrogation cabinets it can't be too serious, and there's no point in starting a panic.'

'Why doesn't Aesop make an announcement?'

'He mightn't think it's worth while.' Surgenor looked along the row again and saw that both Carlen and Gillespie had half-risen from their seats and were frozen in that position, staring at him. 'Let's go to my room and quiz Aesop in private.' He walked to the door of the gallery-like observation chamber followed by Voysey and, at a greater distance, Carlen and Gillespie.

'Where are you guys going?' The voice, laden with discords of nervous stress, belonged to Billy Narvik, a wispy-bearded twenty-year-old, who had joined the *Sarafand* two trips back.

'To have a quiet drink,' Surgenor told him. 'We've seen all this star-jumping stuff before.'

'Don't try to gas me, Dave – you never saw anything like *that* before.' A general murmur of unease followed Narvik's words, and Surgenor wished the youngster would sit down and keep his mouth shut.

'What do you think you saw?'

'I saw three or four jumps, all on top of each other. There were galaxies, nothing *but* galaxies, and now this.' Narvik gestured at the surrounding star fields. 'This isn't the Five Suns group.'

'For your information, Billy,' Surgenor said evenly, 'you didn't see any galaxies, and you can't see any stars now. All this is just a projection that Aesop lays on for our benefit. None of the views that we get in this room have to correspond with what's actually outside the ship.'

'They usually do, don't they?'

'Usually.' Surgenor paused, seeking inspiration. 'But if the new equipment we just got in has some bugs in it we might be seeing part of Aesop's astrogation memory.'

Narvik gave a derisive snort. 'A blind man could see you being tactful, Dave – Aesop has no memory of intergalactic space.'

'How do we know that? All ship computers take their normal-space bearings from the twenty or so galaxies of the Local Group, and Aesop could simulate their . . .'

'You're gassing us again! What do you take me for?' Narvik left his seat and came running, wide-eyed, towards Surgenor. 'What sort of a bloody moron do you think I am?' He began struggling with Sig Carlen and Al Gillespie as they sandwiched him and gripped his arms. A visible wave of unrest swept through the watching company.

'Calm down, everybody,' Surgenor ordered, raising his voice. 'The point is that if there was any kind of a snarl-up in our normal-space or beta-space astrogation systems Aesop would let us know about it, and . . .'

'This is *Sarafand* control making an announcement for the attention of all crew members,' came the omnidirectional voice of Aesop. 'Due to a major malfunction in the ship's astrogation and location control complex, Survey Mission 837/LM/4002a has been aborted.'

110

'We're lost!' somebody shouted. 'Billy was right – we're lost!'

'Don't be so damn childish,' Surgenor bellowed, making himself heard above the uproar. 'Spaceships don't get lost. Listen, everybody – I want you all to calm down and keep quiet while we sort this thing out with Aesop. Now, I'm going to talk to him, and I'm going to do it right here so that everybody will know exactly what's going on. Okay?'

There was a gradual return to silence. Surgenor, now beginning to feel selfconscious, looked up at the ceiling, in the direction of the ship's control levels, then became uncomfortably aware that he had adopted the stance of a man addressing his deity. He lowered his gaze and, resolutely staring straight ahead, began his dialogue with the artificial intelligence upon whose proper functioning all their lives depended.

'Hear these words,' he said slowly. 'Aesop, we saw that the beta-space transition was not completed in a ... normal manner, and there is some confusion in our minds as to exactly what has happened. For a start – for the benefit of the newer members of the crew – I would like you to reassure us about any possibility of the *Sarafand* being lost.'

'If you are applying the word "lost" to a condition of not knowing our position in relation to the standard galactic co-ordinate system, then I can assure you that the *Sarafand* is not lost,' Aesop replied immediately.

Surgenor felt both vindicated and relieved for only an instant before noticing the unusually pedantic nature of Aesop's reply. Struggling to ignore a premonition of disaster, he said, 'Aesop, is there another sense in which the word "lost" *would* apply to our situation?'

There was a brief, but noticeable, hesitation before Aesop said, 'If you define it as meaning "in a condition of irretrievableness" or "not to be recovered" ... then I regret to say that, for all practical purposes, the *Sarafand* is lost.'

'I don't understand that,' Surgenor blurted, breaking a throbbing silence. 'What are you saying to us?'

'The malfunction I have already referred to in the ship's astrogation and location control complex has resulted in a normal-space emergence at a point which is extremely remote from our intended destination.' Aesop spoke in measured, neutral tones, as

111

though announcing a change in the week's breakfast menu.

'We are positioned close to the centre of the galaxy designated as N.5893-278(S) in the Revised Standard Catalogue. Our mean distance from the Local Group – which, of course, includes the Milky Way system and Earth – is approximately thirty million light-years.

'This fact means that we are unable to return to Earth.'

fifteen

The conference was held in the semi-circular mess room, at a table which was plentifully scattered with glasses, cups and ashtrays.

Surgenor had noticed two main types of reaction to Aesop's announcement – some crew members had become intensely animated, alert-eyed and talkative; others had withdrawn to varying degrees, tending to remain silent and to show a broody interest in their own fingernails or in the design of personal artifacts such as cigarette lighters. Christine Holmes was in the latter group, looking ill and tragic. Billy Narvik, having accepted tranquillization, was smiling bemusedly as he stroked his beard. The two other new men – pale, reticent youngsters called John Rizno and Wilbur Desanko – stared about them in mute accusation as though trying to find a human culprit for their misfortune.

Surgenor, who had been tacitly assigned the role of chairman, tapped the long table with his empty whisky glass. 'It occurs to me,' he said slowly, feeling his way, 'that we ought to make sure we're all on the same wavelength. Is there anybody here who thinks Aesop could be wrong? Is there anybody who thinks there *is* a way of getting back home?'

Several men made restless movements.

'Aesop isn't infallible,' Burt Schilling said, glancing at those nearest him. 'I mean, the fact that we're here proves it.'

Surgenor nodded. 'Valid point.'

'I'd like to put it a little more strongly than that,' Theo Mossbake added. 'It seems to me that our so-called Captain Aesop can be downright dumb, and I just don't think we have to accept everything he says like it's the word of God or something.' His voice grew louder. 'All right, so one of his new memory units was faulty and he made a jump into unknown space, outside our galaxy. Why in hell didn't he stop there? Why didn't he just look around, spot our own galaxy, and jump back into it?'

'That's what he tried to do,' Al Gillespie said irritably. 'Aesop has already explained that the beta-space gravitation flux was too high. It was like a strong current carrying us out to sea. From what he said, we could have travelled a lot farther than ... whatever it was ... thirty million light-years.'

'At least we can still *see* the Local Group,' Surgenor said without thinking, and was immediately sorry he had spoken.

'That's great. That's a big consolation to all of us,' Schilling said. 'When we start getting hungry we can take turns around the telescope admiring the Local Group. Waving to our friends.'

'This is a conference,' Surgenor told him. 'Save the sarcasm and self-pity for your own room. Okay?'

'No, it isn't okay.' Schilling stared resentfully at Surgenor, a vein pulsing in his throat. 'Who do you think you are, anyway?' He began to rise to his feet, and Surgenor felt a pang of shameful joy at the prospect of discharging his own tensions so simply and so naturally, merely by clubbing another human being with his fist.

Mossbake caught Schilling's upper arm and pulled him down into his seat. 'My training was mostly in the hotel business ... I was doing the minimum two-year stint with the CS to raise some capital ... so I don't know much about beta-space physics,' Mossbank said. 'But I understand the analogy that Al used, the one about a current taking us out to sea. What I'd like to know is – can't we tack against the current? Is there no way of zigzagging back the way we came?'

Gillespie leaned forward. 'In a ship specially designed and equipped for that sort of thing it might be possible. But Aesop reckons there would be upwards of two hundred beta-space jumps involved, providing we didn't hit a region where conditions were worse – and our fuel capsules are good for thirty at the outside. There's the time factor, as well. Without any beta-space charts to help him, Aesop would have to do a major four-pi survey before each jump, and a job like that can take up to four days. Multiply it out and you get a journey time of over two years – and we've got food for a month.'

'I see,' Mossbake said quietly. 'It's funny I didn't think of food –

with my catering experience, too. Does that mean we just . . . starve?'

The twelve seated at the table changed their attitude slightly, as though they had been joined by an invisible thirteenth presence, and Surgenor decided the time had come, once again, for him to go into his act. In two decades of survey work he had almost perfected the Surgenor image of the big rock-steady man, experienced, imperturbable, slow to anger, possessing reserves of every kind of strength. In a way, he sometimes stood in for the ship itself, presenting – as had already happened within the hour – a human target for the frustration which other crewmen would like to have vented on Aesop. It was a part he had once enjoyed playing, in the days when it had still been possible to deceive himself, but of late it had grown onerous and he had a yearning to retire from the stage . . .

'Starve?' Surgenor looked at Mossbake in a kind of humorous surprise. 'You can starve if that's what you really want to do, but there's a galaxy out there with a lot of planets in it, and a lot of untouched food on those planets – and I'm going to eat my way through one of them. Or a good part of it, anyway.'

'You're not worried about not getting back home?'

'No. I would prefer to go back – it would be crazy to pretend anything else – but if I can't make it back I'm going to go on living somewhere else. It's a hell of a sight better than being . . .' Surgenor broke off as Billy Narvik, who was at the opposite end of the table, gave a sudden bark of laughter.

'I'm sorry,' Narvik said, still grinning with drugged benevolence, as he saw that he had become the focus of attention. 'I apologize for interrupting the proceedings, but you guys are *so* funny.'

'In what way?' Mike Targett said, speaking for the first time.

'This conference . . . You're sitting around – all so serious – counting up fuel capsules and cans of beans, and nobody has even *mentioned* the one really important commodity, the only one that matters a damn.'

'What is it?'

'Her!' Narvik pointed at Christine Holmes, who was sitting directly across the table from him. 'The only female we've got.'

Surgenor tapped the table with his glass. 'I don't think you're in any condition to take part in this meeting, Billy – and we're talking about survival.'

'What do you think I'm talking about, for God's sake?' Narvik looked about him with calm eyes. 'Survival of the species! We have one female, and – I'm sorry if this offends any sensibilities – but it seems to me that we have to decide how to make the best use of her.'

Sig Carlen got to his feet and moved to a position behind Narvik's chair, shoulder muscles spread. 'Are we agreed that friend Narvik should lie down in his room for a while?'

'That won't change anything,' Narvik said pleasantly. 'This is a whole new ball game, folks, and the sooner we lay down the rules the better it'll be for everybody.'

Surgenor nodded to Carlen, who slipped his hands under Narvik's arms and began lifting him out of his chair. Narvik resisted only passively, by slumping like a drunk.

'Leave him alone,' Schilling cut in. 'He's talking sense, isn't he? If we have to make a new start in this galaxy we'll have to face up to certain facts and get used to new ways of thinking, and I for one . . .'

'You for one,' Carlen interrupted, 'might have to get used to new ways of eating – without your teeth, for example.'

Schilling responded by baring his teeth and pinching one between forefinger and thumb. 'I've got good teeth, Sig. I don't think you could even loosen them.'

'I'll be helping him,' Victor Voysey said, his freckled face sombre. 'And I use an axle wrench.'

'You can take your . . .'

'That's enough!' Surgenor made no attempt to hide his anger. 'Narvik was right when he said this is a whole new ball game, and here is one of the ground rules – Chris Holmes is to be a fully private, autonomous individual. We can't exist any other way.'

'We won't exist at all, before long, unless we're realistic about breeding,' Schilling said doggedly.

Surgenor stared at him in open dislike. 'Could it be that you consider yourself prime breeding stock?'

'Better'n you, big Dave. At least I'm still . . .'

'*Gentlemen!*' Christine Holmes got to her feet amid an abrupt silence and looked around the table, her strong-jawed face white with strain, then gave a shaky laugh. 'Did I say gentlemen? I'm sorry – I'll start again. Bastards. If you bastards don't mind I'd like to show you something which has a bearing on the discussion – and you'd better look at it carefully, because this is the only chance you're going to get.'

She gripped her clothing with both hands, pulling the uniform blouse upwards and the top of her slacks downwards to expose a flat abdomen which was puckered with surgical scars. Surgenor looked at her dark-shadowed eyes and felt that in the past twenty years he had been nowhere, had learned very little.

'There's nothing in there shipmates. No works, no bits and pieces – they've all been taken away,' Christine said. 'Can everybody see?'

'There's no need for this,' Schilling muttered, turning his gaze away.

'Ah, but there is! You're the one who was talking about facing up to the facts – and this is a fact, sonny.' Christine forced her voice into normal conversational tones, and even managed to smile as she rearranged her clothing and sat down.

She interlaced her fingers and glanced around the table. 'I hope I haven't shocked any of free-thinking pioneers, but I thought it best to prove that you can class me as one of the boys. It makes things simpler, doesn't it?'

'Very much simpler,' Surgenor said at once, anxious to drive the episode into the past. 'Perhaps now we can get on with the business of agreeing the instructions we're going to give Aesop.'

'I didn't even know we could instruct Aesop,' Carlen said, releasing the now-quiescent Narvik and returning to his seat.

'Our present situation is way outside his terms of reference, so this is where we need the flexible human response the union execs keep talking about.'

'We wouldn't need it if we weren't here in the first place.'

'I'm not getting involved in that one.' Surgenor kept his eyes away from Christine as he spoke. 'Now, we have to agree that we stay in this galaxy – which seems as good as any of the billions of others out there. We have to instruct Aesop to check out the region for suitable, planet-bearing suns. Then we have to decide on a food rationing system to extend our supplies.' Jotting notes on a memo pad, Surgenor droned his way through a short list of proposals, trying to make them sound commonplace, hoping that what they had done to Christine would be equally reduced and made unmemorable.

The sub-committee appointed to select a destination sun consisted of Surgenor, Al Gillespie and Mike Targett. Surgenor was mildly

116

surprised at how easy it had been to get the sort of group he wanted, and guessed that the incipient faction headed by Burt Schilling were glad to get away from the table until the ripples of the Christine Holmes incident would have had time to fade.

Equipping themselves with notepads and pencils, the trio moved into the observation room and sat down amid a plenum of stars. The distribution of suns around the *Sarafand* was so uniform, and their brightness so intense, that the three men appeared to be perched on a dangerous gallery spanning an abyss.

'I've never seen anything quite like this before,' Gillespie commented. 'There must be a thousand or more suns within a radius of ten light-years. You could almost find planetary systems with a pair of field glasses.'

'Slight exaggeration,' Targett said, 'but I see what you mean. It's about time we had some luck.'

'Luck?' Surgenor cleared his throat. 'Hear these words, Aesop. Did you have any control over our point of emergence in this galaxy?'

'Yes, David. This globular cluster was a conspicuous object, even in beta-space. I had enough residual control to ensure that the ship emerged near its centre.' Aesop's pervasive voice seemed to emanate from space itself.

'You knew we'd be looking for a planet to settle on?'

'That was the logical assumption.'

'I see.' Surgenor glanced significantly at his two companions. 'Aesop, we now require from you a complete survey of the cluster with the object of locating the suns most likely to have Earth-type planets. Results in print-out form. Four copies. How long will that take?'

'Approximately five hours.'

'That is satisfactory.' It suddenly came to Surgenor that he was exhausted, that there was nothing he could usefully do in the next five hours, and that he could no longer put off the first moment when he would find himself alone in his room, isolated, thirty million light-years from Earth. The alternative was to have another drink, but he had no wish to start using alcohol as a crutch – especially as the supply would run out in a few weeks.

'I suppose we'd better get some rest,' he said to Gillespie and Targett, glancing at his watch. 'We can meet here at . . .'

'I have carried out a preliminary spectroscopic survey of the cluster,' Aesop cut in unexpectedly. 'The emission lines prove that the stellar matter has the same composition as is found in the home galaxy, but in every case the lines are shifted towards the blue end of the spectrum.'

Without knowing why, Surgenor felt a spasm of alarm. 'That doesn't reduce the possibility of finding suitable planets, does it?'

'No.' Aesop's reply was comforting, but made his intervention more puzzling.

Surgenor frowned at Targett, who was known to have some formal grounding in astronomy. 'What made Aesop tell us that?'

'Blue shift?' Targett looked as puzzled as Surgenor felt. 'I guess it means that all the stars in this cluster are moving towards us. Not towards *us* – towards a common centre which we happen to be near.'

'So what?'

Targett raised his shoulders, looking blank. 'It's unusual, that's all. You usually find that everything is expanding.'

'Aesop, we note what you say about the shifting of spectral lines,' Surgenor said. 'It means that this cluster is imploding, right?'

'That is correct. The velocity of the stars near the central region is upwards of one hundred and fifty kilometres a second, and it gets higher towards the edge of the cluster. I informed you about the phenomenon because it has no known parallel in the Milky Way system.'

Surgenor developed an uneasy feeling that something important was being left unsaid, and yet he knew that – regardless of how many subtleties had been built into Aesop's "personality" – his designers had never intended him to exhibit coyness.

'All right,' he said, 'so we're in an imploding cluster, and that's a new kind of phenomenon in our experience – but if our previous experience is limited to the Milky Way system aren't we bound to get a few surprises in other parts of the universe?'

'The viewpoint you express is philosophically valid,' Aesop replied. 'However, the truly surprising thing about this star cluster is not its configuration in space, but in time.'

'Aesop, I don't understand that. Make it simpler.'

'The stars in the cluster have a mean separation of one-point-two light-years. They are moving towards the centre at a rate of about one hundred and fifty kilometres a second. We are already at or near the centre of the cluster, but we can detect no stellar collisions or central mass. The implication is that we have reached our present position less than one hundred and fifty Earth years before the first collision – but astronomical time-scales are such that this implication should be rejected.'

'You mean it's impossible?'

'It is not impossible,' Aesop replied blandly. 'But on an astronomical time-scale the period of one hundred and fifty years is vanishingly small. I have insufficient data about local conditions to be able to calculate the probabilities, but it is extremely unlikely that we should have arrived here at this stage in the cluster's evolution. Either the cluster should be very much larger and more diffuse, or there should be a central mass.'

Surgenor stared at the crowded, fiercely glowing sky. 'Then . . . what's your explanation?'

'I have no explanation, David. I am merely advising you of the facts.'

'In that case we have to assume that we arrived here at an interesting time,' Surgenor said. 'The improbable is bound to happen every now and . . .'

'Aesop,' Targett said urgently, 'we're not on the edge of a black hole, are we?'

'No. A black hole is easily detectable, both in normal-space and in beta-space, and I would have made certain to avoid it. In fact, I am unable to detect even a moderate gravity generator in the region – which makes the condensation of the cluster harder to explain.'

'Mmm. You said the stars nearer the outside of the cluster are moving faster, Aesop. Is their speed proportionate to the distance from the centre?'

'A random sample indicates that is the case.'

'That's strange,' Targett said thoughtfully. 'It's almost as if . . .' His voice faded away as he examined the surrounding star fields with renewed interest.

'What were you going to say?' Gillespie prompted.

'Nothing. I get crazy ideas sometimes.'

'We're not getting anywhere with this discussion.' Surgenor looked at his watch, which had been adjusted to ship time. 'I suggest we break it up for a while and meet here again at seven. We might have our heads cleared by that time, and there'll be Aesop's report to work on.'

The others nodded their assent and they moved back into the brightly lit normality of the mess room, away from the psychological pressures of the alien sky. Surgenor went up the main companionway to the next deck and entered the bow-shaped corridor of the sleeping quarters. For the sake of administrative convenience, the crew were assigned rooms in accordance with the numbers of their survey modules, and, as the occupant of the left-hand seat in *Module Five*, Surgenor lived in the ninth.

He was passing the first room, where for the past five years he had been accustomed to stop for jawing sessions with Marc Lamereux, when it occurred to him that he owed Christine Holmes an apology. The door was closed, but its do-not-disturb bezel was dark, making it impossible to tell if she was inside at that moment. He hesitated, then tapped the plastic panel and heard an indistinct reply which sounded like an invitation to enter. Surgenor turned the handle, opened the door and was greeted by a flurry of movement and startled swearing. Christine, naked to the waist, was sitting on the edge of the bed with her arms crossed over her breasts.

'Sorry!' Surgenor closed the door and waited in the corridor, beginning to wish he had gone straight to his room.

'What's the idea?' Christine had pulled on her uniform blouse when she opened the door. 'What do you want?'

Surgenor tried to smile. 'Aren't you going to invite me in?'

'What do you want?' she repeated impatiently, ignoring his suggestion.

'Well ... I was going to apologize.'

'What for?'

'For what happened at the meeting. And I guess I haven't helped much, either.'

'I don't need any help. Turkeys like Narvik and Schilling don't bother me.'

'I dare say they don't, but that's not the point.'

'Isn't it?' She sighed and he caught the tang of tobacco smoke on her breath. 'All right – you've apologized, and that makes everybody feel better. Now, do you mind if I get some rest?' She closed the door and there came the sound of the lock being operated more firmly than was necessary. The do-not-disturb bezel began to glow.

Surgenor thoughtfully stroked his jaw as he continued along the corridor to his own room. When Christine Holmes was angry, as she undoubtedly still was, she could be as tough and abrasive as any man, but in the moment of being taken unawares she had reacted in a classically feminine manner. The ancient defensive gesture, the screening of the breasts from strange eyes, seemed to indicate sexuality, to show that in spite of everything she regarded herself as essentially female. Surgenor tried to imagine the Christine he knew – big-boned, sallow-complexioned, hard-handed, smoking, ready to take on a male world on its own terms – as the person she might once have been before life had started wielding the big stick, but he was unable to come up with a different picture. Recognizing the futility of the exercise, he put her out of his mind as he entered his own room.

Kicking off his boots, he lay down on the bed and allowed himself to think about being stranded thirty million light-years from home. Was it any worse than being stranded one light-year from home? Rationally – no; but there was more to life than rationality. He did not exist as a pure intellect, and the coldness of the intergalactic gulf had seeped into his bones, into his guts, and he could feel it laying waste to his spirit, and he was unable to see how he would ever again be able to laugh, or sleep easily, or renew himself at the fountains of human friendship.

sixteen

The print-out listed five G2 suns – all within a radius of six light-years – whose gravitational profiles showed the complexities caused by planets. One of them, designated as Prospect One by Aesop, appeared to have as many as thirty worlds swarming around it like electrons in a shell.

'That makes things simple,' Surgenor said, looking at the star which Aesop had enclosed in a pulsing green circle. 'The sooner we get to Prospect One and start checking out the living accommodation the better it'll be.'

Gillespie nodded. 'There's a lot of booze being shifted in the mess room.'

Surprisingly Mike Targett looked doubtful. 'I'm not so sure about the whole programme Aesop has set out. I've been thinking things over all afternoon, and something tells me we should get out of this cluster altogether and start from scratch somewhere else.'

'*Something* tells you? We need more authority than that, Mike. It isn't going to bother any of us if there are a few big bangs around here in a century or two.'

'I know, but . . .' Targett hunched broodily in his chair, staring over the edge of the catwalk which seemed to bridge eternity. 'I get a feeling there's something really weird about this region.'

Surgenor recalled that Mike Targett, hard-headed young gambler, was not the sort of person to be influenced by moods or mysticism. 'But it Aesop thinks it's all right . . .'

'Aesop is a computer – as I know better than anybody else – and he is programmed. Admittedly, his programmes are big, subtle, sophisticated, open-ended, self-expanding, anything else you can think of, but they're still programmes and therefore only equip him to deal with the *conceivable*. Faced with the inconceivable, Aesop can't be relied on.'

'What's so inconceivable about a condensing cluster?'

'How can I answer that?' Targett replied. 'But for all we know we've strayed into a zone of time reversal. Perhaps the cluster is actually expanding when seen in normal time.'

'Now, *that's* inconceivable – so much so that I couldn't swallow it.'

'We'd be able to detect the remains of the central explosion,' Gillespie said.

'Would we? With our basic constants no longer . . .' Targett broke off and gave a wry smile. 'I don't believe we're in a zone of time reversal, either – I was only trying to give you an example of something outside Aesop's areas of competence.'

Surgenor cleared his throat significantly. 'We're wasting time, Mike. Unless you can come up with a more concrete objection, I'm going to move that we take Prospect One as our next destination.'

'I've said my piece.'

'That's it then,' Gillespie said. 'I vote for Prospect One, as well, so

122

let's get the show on the road. I'll round up the others while you're telling Aesop.'

The twelve chairs in the observation room were filled within a short time. Now that the initial shock had passed and there had been a period of adjustment, the crew members' true reactions to their predicament were becoming apparent. Some were drinking hard to maintain a kind of grim joviality, some were watchful yet withdrawn, and others kept up a purposeful bustle of activity. The general atmosphere was one of calmness in the face of crisis, something for which Surgenor was grateful, even though he suspected that to some extent it had been brought about by Aesop. If tranquillizers had been introduced into the food and water it had been done discreetly and effectively.

Surgenor kept his gaze on the target star, mentally bracing himself for the instant in which it would be transformed from a distant point of light into the blinding disc of a nearby sun. The range was less than four light-years, which meant that Aesop should be able to take them right into the multi-world system in a single accurately judged leap. This was one of the reasons he had preferred to stay in a densely packed star cluster – most of the journey time on any mission was used up in the normal-space approaches to planets, and where food supplies were limited there was an advantage in making very short, very precise leaps right into the hearts of target systems.

As the seconds ticked by Surgenor felt the familiar build-up of excitement that always preceded the near-miracle of a beta-space jump. On this occasion, perhaps because so much depended on the outcome, the wait seemed more prolonged than usual, the tension more unbearable. Surgenor forced himself to sit without fidgeting, apparently at ease, while he struggled to relate subjective and objective time; not until he saw both Gillespie and Voysey glancing at their watches did he acknowledge a growing conviction that – monstrously unfair it might seem – something else had gone wrong on board the *Sarafand*.

'Do you think we should quiz Aesop?' Gillespie whispered from the seat beside him.

'If there's any kind of hold-up he's bound to . . .' The sound of the chime which always preceded a general announcement froze Surgenor to silence.

123

'I must inform all those present,' came Aesop's voice, 'that it is not possible for the ship to complete the scheduled beta-space transition to Prospect One.'

There was an immediate ripple of surprise and annoyance, above which several men could be heard demanding an explanation. None of them seemed particularly alarmed, and Surgenor began to wonder if all his foreboding about a jackpot trip had made him unduly pessimistic.

'The reason we are unable to make the transition is that my beta-space sensors are supplying me with data which I cannot accept.' Aesop had adjusted the volume of his voice to make himself heard above the general noise level.

'Be more precise, Aesop,' Voysey called.

'As you will know, if you have studied your CS indoctrination books, a beta-space jump is completed in stages. In the first stage a sensor unit is rotated through five-space into beta-space, then is brought back after it has surveyed and recorded the graviton flux. As soon as its readings have been correlated with normal-space astrogation data – in other words, as soon as the target star has been identified and located – the entire ship is rotated into beta-space, the correct impulsion is applied, and the ship is then rotated back into normal-space in the vicinity of the target star.'

'I know all that stuff,' Voysey said peevishly. 'Get to the point, Aesop.'

'I have already made my point, Victor, but for your benefit I will explain the situation again.' The hint of reproof in Aesop's voice caused Voysey to glance sideways at the men nearest him and pull a face.

'The ship's astrogation system has a series of built-in blocks which prevent a jump from being carried out until I am satisfied that I know where we are jumping *to*. I am unable to locate our destination in beta-space – and, therefore, the ship is unable to move.'

'Is *that* all that's wrong?' Ray Kessler said, breaking the ensuing silence. 'Well, hurry up and get a bead on Prospect One, Aesop. It's almost in our laps, isn't it?' He pointed at the brilliant star within its pulsing green circle. While he was speaking, the cold of the starless intergalactic deep, which had been dormant inside Surgenor, began to stir within him and spread its black tentacles.

'The fact that a stellar object is readily identifiable in normal-

124

space does not mean that it can be easily identifiable in beta-space,' Aesop replied. 'There is no light or any other form of electromagnetic radiation in beta-space. Astrogation is carried out by sensing and analysing the flow patterns of gravitons emitted by stellar masses. Gravitons are difficult to perceive, and their courses are not predictable. To quote the analogy used in your indoctrination books, the beta-space traveller is like a blind man in a large draughty room in which a number of people are blowing soap bubbles. He has to find his way, correctly, from one person to another – and all he has to guide him is the incidence of bubbles breaking on his skin.'

'So what's the problem now? Can't you feel the bubbles?'

'Not in any useful manner. The graviton, the gravity quantum, was believed to be a universal constant, but in this region of space it appears to be variable which increases with time.'

'Aesop!' Mike Targett had leapt to his feet, his eyes fixed on Surgenor's face. 'Is it a local condition? Confined to this cluster?'

'That conclusion is in agreement with the evidence I have.'

'Then get us out of here, for Christ's sake! Make a blind jump. To anywhere!'

There was a pause before Aesop replied, time enough for the numbing, sterilizing coldness to reach Surgenor's brain.

'I repeat, the astrogation system has a series of built-in blocks which prevent a jump from being carried out until the destination has been selected and verified. It is impossible for me to select a destination – therefore, the ship cannot move.'

Targett shook his head, refusing to believe. 'But that's only a mechanical thing, a safety procedure – we can override it.'

'It is one of the most basic design parameters of the ship's control system. To alter it one would have to redesign and rebuild the central control unit – a task which would require a high degree of specialized knowledge, plus the resources of a large production plant.' Once again, the bland and pedantic tones of Aesop's voice had no correspondence with the burden of his meaning, and Surgenor – his mind ricocheting away into allegory – conceived a fantastic image of a judge putting on a red nose to pronounce a death sentence.

'I see.' Targett gazed around the ship's company, gave them a thin, unnatural smile and walked out in the direction of the mess.

'What were you characters talking about?' Kessler demanded. 'What's going on here?'

'I'll tell you,' Burt Schilling put in, his voice blurred with panic. 'They say the ship can't move. That's right, isn't it, big Dave?'

Surgenor stood up, glancing after Targett. 'It's a bit early to jump to conclusions.'

'Don't try to gas *me*, you big bastard.' Schilling came towards Surgenor, jabbing an accusing finger. 'You know we're stuck here. Come on – admit it.'

Surgenor realized that the familiar transference had occurred, that – as had happened in the past – he was being identified with the ship and its nonexistent captain. But now he had no reserves upon which others could draw.

'I've nothing to admit,' he growled at Schilling. 'You have the same access to Aesop as anybody else – talk to him about it.' He turned to go after Mike Targett.

'I'm talking to *you*!' Schilling clawed at Surgenor's right arm, pulling him back. Surgenor, instead of resisting the drag of the younger man's hands, allowed his arm to swing back freely, then threw his own strength into the sweeping movement. Taken by surprise, Schilling stumbled backwards, struck the low parapet of the observation area and fell, screaming, towards the stars. A second later he landed on the curved projection screen. An automatic switch brought on lights and the stars paled to invisibility on the inner surface of a glassy grey sphere. Schilling, who appeared to be winded but not seriously hurt, lay clutching his stomach and staring up at Surgenor with slit-eyed hatred.

'When junior recovers from his little accident,' Surgenor said to the watching group, 'tell him to take up his complaints with Aesop – I've got problems of my own.'

Theo Mossbake cleared his throat. 'Are we really stuck?'

'That's the way it looks right now, but with rationing we can make our feed last three months, if not longer. That's quite a bit of time to try working something out.'

'But if the ship can't be . . .'

'*Talk to Aesop!*' Surgenor turned and strode out of the observation room and into the deserted mess, breathing heavily. He went to the drinks dispenser, drew himself a glass of iced water and drank it slowly, then climbed the companionway. The door to the fifth room was closed, but not locked. Surgenor tapped it gently and spoke Targett's name. There was no reply, and after waiting a few seconds he pushed the door open. Mike Targett was sitting on the edge of his bed, shoulders hunched. His forehead was glistening with sweat and his eyes were dull, but otherwise he appeared normal and in control of himself.

'I haven't decided to end it all, if that's what's worrying you,' he said.

'I'm glad about that.' Surgenor tapped the door jamb. 'Mind if I come in?'

'Sure, but I told you I'm all right.'

Surgenor entered the room and closed the door behind him. 'Okay, young Mike – out with it.'

Targett looked up at him with the same unnatural smile as before. 'I could do you a big favour and not tell you this.'

'No favours – just talk.'

'Okay, Dave.' Targett paused to gather his thoughts. 'You've heard of pulsars, quasars, mythars, block holes, white holes, time windows – right?'

'Right.'

'But you've never heard about dwindlars.'

'Dwindlars?' Surgenor frowned at him. 'Can't say I have.'

'That's because I've just invented the word. It's a new term for a new astronomical phenomenom. New to us, anyway.'

'What happens in it?'

Targett's smile wavered. 'What does the name suggest to you?'

'Dwindlar? Well, the only thing I can ...'

'I got the first inkling today when Aesop mentioned that the velocities of the stars in the cluster appeared to be proportionate to their distance from the centre. We see the outermost stars approaching fastest, and so on.'

'We already knew we were in an imploding cluster,' Surgenor said, still puzzled.

'Ah, but that's the whole point – we *aren't*.' Some animation returned to Targett's eyes. 'I'm glad I managed to work this out – the whole notion of a star cluster falling in on itself was an offence to reason.'

'Are you saying that Aesop's instruments are wrong? That the stars in this cluster aren't moving in towards the centre?'

127

'Not quite. What I'm saying is that no matter where you went in the cluster, no matter where you carried out your observations from, you would find that the stars appeared to be moving towards you, with the most distant moving fastest.'

Surgenor shifted his weight. 'Mike, does that make sense?'

'Unfortunately – yes. Long-range astronomy has always been familiar with this type of effect, only in reverse. When an astronomer measures the speeds of distant galaxies, he always finds that the most distant ones are retreating fastest – but it isn't because he's positioned at a real central point. In an expanding universe, everything moves outward uniformly from everything else – and – by simple arithmetic – the farther an object is from an observer, the faster it will appear to be retreating from him.'

'That's in an *expanding* universe,' Surgenor said slowly, his thoughts beginning to leap ahead. 'Are we . . .'

'The evidence is that we've jumped into the centre of a contracting volume of space. That's why there are so many suns packed so close together. The space between them is shrinking. The suns themselves are shrinking. *We* must be shrinking, Dave.'

Surgenor glanced involuntarily at his own hands before his common sense asserted itself. 'That doesn't make sense. In an expanding system our bodies didn't get bigger – and even if they had done it wouldn't have made any difference . . .' He stopped speaking as he saw Targett was shaking his head.

'We're in a different kind of set-up,' Targett said. 'It's not as if somebody had grabbed a big gear lever and thrown the entire cosmos into reverse. We're in a kind of inclusion – like a diamond in a rock, or a bubble in a glass paperweight – only a few tens of light-years across, and *everything* in it is shrinking. And that includes us.'

'But there's no way to know that. Our measuring rules would be shrinking at exactly the same rate as everything we tried to measure, so . . .'

'Except gravitons, Dave. The gravity quantum *is* a universal constant. Even here.'

Surgenor thought again, trying to adapt to alien concepts. 'Aesop said it was an increasing variable.'

'*Appeared* to be an increasing variable. That's because we're getting smaller, and that's what screwed up his whole astrogation and control complex.'

Surgenor sat down on the room's only chair. 'If all this is true, doesn't it mean we're making progress? If Aesop now knows that the problem is ...'

'There isn't time Dave.' Targett leaned back on his bed, stared at the ceiling and spoke in a dreamy, almost peaceful voice. 'In just over two hours from now we'll all be dead.'

seventeen

The sound of a woman's voice raised in anger was followed by a man's hoarse sobbing and an irregular clamour of footsteps. Surgenor ran to the door of his own room, threw it open and saw Billy Narvik and Christine Holmes locked together in struggle a short distance along the corridor. Her blouse had been partially torn open and her face was haggard with fury. Narvik, who was grappling with her from behind, had a dark stain around his mouth and his eyes showed only the whites beneath tremulant lids. His face was ecstatic.

'Let go of her, Billy,' Surgenor ordered. 'You know this isn't a good idea.'

'I can handle this little tick,' Christine said in a bitter monotone. She was kicking back at Narvik's shins, her heel connecting solidly every time, but he appeared not to notice. Surgenor moved in close, caught hold of Narvik's wrists and tried to force them apart.

Suddenly aware of a third presence, Narvik widened his eyes and the lines of his face altered as he saw Surgenor. 'Stay out of this, big Dave,' he panted. 'I want this, and I've got to ... There's nothing else left.'

Christine renewed her struggles to break free as Surgenor increased the outward pull on Narvik's wrists. The smaller man was surprisingly strong and to break his hold Surgenor had to bend his own knees and lower himself into a position from which he could

129

exert maximum effort. This brought his face almost into contact with Christine's and he felt the pressure of her hips against his as the unnatural intimacy was prolonged. The trio remained in a strained equilibrium for several seconds, then Narvik's arms began to weaken.

'Dave, *Dave!*' Narvik began a conspiratorial pleading as his grip was finally broken. 'You don't understand, man – it's years since I've managed to ...'

He fell silent as Christine ducked out of the cincture of arms, spun round and in the same movement struck him a loose-fingered blow across the mouth. Surgenor released Narvik's wrists, allowing him to shrink away against the curving wall of the corridor. Narvik pressed the back of a hand to his lips and gazed accusingly from Surgenor to Christine.

'I get it! I get it' Narvik gave a quavering laugh. 'But it's only for two hours. What use is two hours to anybody?' He walked away in the direction of the companionway, moving with an incongruously dignified gait.

'You shouldn't have hit him,' Surgenor said. 'You can tell he's been chewing some kind of weed.'

'That makes rape all right, does it?' Christine began fastening her blouse.

'I didn't say that,' Surgenor stared at her in frustration, obscurely angry because she had remained as she was, because she had failed to metamorphose in some indefinable way which would have helped him to see a purpose in life or meaning in death. It had seemed to him that, with a term of two hours placed on their existence, it was the duty of the crew members to transcend their old selves and thus, if only in token, make the short time that remained worth putting in the scales against the decades they were being denied. He knew it had been a straightforward fear reaction, that his subconscious – in an effort to deny the facts – was setting up spurious short-range goals, but a part of him clung obstinately to the notion, and he still wished that Christine would be what she could be.

'I'm going to my room,' she said. 'And this time I'll make sure the door is locked.'

'It might be better to be with somebody.'

She shook her head. 'You do it your way, and I'll do it mine.'

130

'Sure.' Surgenor was trying to think of something worth adding when he heard a commotion break out in the mess room below, and felt an abrupt wave-crash of surprise and alarm. Force of habit caused him to sprint to the companionway and half-run, half-slither down it. The group of men who had chosen to drink themselves into oblivion were positioned in different parts of the mess, some of them already stupefied, but all had their eyes fixed on the head of the metal stair which led down to the hangar deck.

Surgenor strode to the stairwell, leaned over the rail and saw Billy Narvik's body lying on the floor below. It was distorted and deathly still, the only movement being that of two rivulets of blood which were groping their way out from beneath the body like furtive tentacles.

'He was trying to fly,' somebody breathed. 'I swear he thought he could fly.'

'That's one way out,' another man said, 'but I think I'll wait.'

Surgenor went on down the stair and knelt beside Narvik's body, confirming what he already knew. The *Sarafand*'s induced gravity system did not produce a full 1G of acceleration in a falling body, but the impact on the metal floor had been enough to break Narvik's neck. Surgenor looked about him at the survey modules in their stalls, then up at the faces visible at the top of the stairwell.

'Will somebody give me a hand to move him?' he said. 'He's dead.'

'It isn't worth it,' Burt Schilling replied. 'He won't be there for long anyway.'

The men leaning on the handrail moved away. Surgenor hesitated, knowing that Schilling was right, but unwilling to leave the remains of a human being crumpled on the hangar floor like so much machine shop waste. He took hold of Narvik's wrists and hauled the body towards the store room which was built into the massive column forming the ship's spine. As he opened the door, lights came on automatically. He espied the circular alloy plate, flush mounted in the floor, scribed with radial lines which marked the ship's centre of gravity and major axes for the benefit of structures teams. In his state of mind it seemed to have an appropriately symbolic or ceremonial appearance. He dragged the body on to it and left the store room, closing the door behind him.

131

'Hear these words, Aesop,' he said.

'I'm listening to you, David.' The voice emanated from the dimness all round.

'Billy Narvik fell down the stair to the hangar deck a couple of minutes ago. I've examined him – and he's dead. I've put the body in the hangar deck tool store, and I'm requesting you to keep that door locked.'

'If that is what you want, I have no objection.' There followed the faint sound of solenoid bolts slipping into place, directed from Aesop's central units far above.

Surgenor went back upstairs and, ignoring several offers of drinks, passed through the mess and climbed to the deck above. He found Christine standing at the top of the steps, smoking a cigarette, one hip casually upthrust as if she was posing for a dude ranch photograph. Again, he felt an irrational anger.

'Did you hear all that?' he said, keeping his voice calm.

'Most of it.' She eyed him impassively through a filigree of smoke.

'You won't have to worry about Billy Narvik again.'

'I wasn't worried about him in the first place.'

'Bully for you.' Surgenor slipped past her, went to his room and locked the door. He threw himself on the bed and at once his mind was drawn back into the whirlpool of confused speculation.

The ultimate jackpot, he knew, eventually came up for everybody – and in rare moments of spiritual malaise he had tried to predict how his own turn might come about. Life in the Cartographical Service was not particularly hazardous, but it offered a great deal of variety, a multitude of ways for the wheels of chance to judder to a halt and lock on to the combination which signified the end of the game for yet another player. He had visualized freakish mechanical failures in his survey module, the risks of contracting exotic diseases, the ironic possibility that he might become a traffic casualty back on Earth – but not even in nightmare had he foreseen anything like the prospect which now lay before him.

After his initial talk with Mike Targett, he had retired to his room and had conferred privately with Aesop. In the churchly solitude, free from the distractions the other crew members would have created, he had been able to absorb the news that Aseop was establishing a set of physical laws for the inverted microcosm. The laws were few in number, reflecting the paucity of data, but the third one had profound implications. It stated, simply, that the rate of shrinkage of any body within a dwindlar was inversely proportional to its mass.

In specific, practical terms this meant that a sun would take many millions of years to achieve zero dimensions – but that the same fate would overtake a body the size of a spaceship in less that one day. The exponential equations derived by Aesop from successive graviton measurements indicated that at 21.37 the *Sarafand* and all its crew would cease to exist.

Surgenor stared at the ceiling of his room and tried to comprehend what Aesop had told him.

The clock on his wall recorded a time of 20.02 hours, which meant there were roughly ninety minutes left. It also meant, by Aesop's reckoning, that the *Sarafand* – once a metal pyramid eighty metres high – had been reduced to the size of a child's toy. The proposition that the entire ship was no larger than a paperweight outraged Surgenor's mind, and the corollary that his own body had been reduced in proportion engendered both terror and disbelief.

There had to be a reasonable limit, he assured himself, to what could be deduced from a couple of astrophysical measurements. After all, what hard facts were there to go on? All right, the light from the stars in the cluster exhibited some degree of blue shift, and Aesop – a computer proven to be fallible by the ship's very own presence in this part of the universe – said it showed the stars were moving inwards. But did it? Was it not a fact that nobody had ever actually measured the speed of a star or a galaxy, and that the whole conceptual edifice of expanding or contracting systems depended on the *interpretation* of red or blue shift as a Doppler effect? Had anybody ever proved that interpretation to be correct? Beyond any doubt?

Surgenor gave a numb, humourless smile as he realized he had been driven to pitting his sketchy knowledge of formal astronomy against the awful powers of Aesop's data banks and processing units. All he had proved was that he was so afraid of what lay ahead that he was beginning to fantasize. The realities of the situation were that he had stayed in the Service too long, that he had travelled too far, that he had run out of time, that it was too late for him to cease being a wilful stranger, that he would never make the real meaningful journeys embarked on by those who remain in one chosen place long enough to know the tilted seasons, that he was totally alone and would be for the rest of his life, that it had all been one ghastly mistake, and that there was no longer any damned thing he could do about it . . .

The red-glowing digits of the clock continued to flicker, squandering Surgenor's life, and he watched them in bleak fascination. An occasional raucus laugh or the sound of a glass shattering reached him from the mess room, but their frequency diminished as his vigil wore on and he knew the alcohol was taking effect. Some of the crew had elected to spend their final hour in the observation chamber. The idea of joining them recurred several times, but that would have involved making a decision and implementing it, and the effort seemed too great. A merciful torpor had settled over him, turning his limbs to unfeeling lead, slowing his mental processes to the point at which it took him a full minute to complete a single thought.

I . . . have . . . seen . . . too . . . many . . . stars.

The gentle tapping on his door struck Surgenor as being something related to another place and time. He listened to it, uncomprehending, then glanced at the clock. Twenty minutes left. He arose with an effort, walked to the door and fumbled it open. Christine Holmes was standing in the corridor, looking at him with pain-filled, puzzled eyes.

'I think I made a mistake,' she said in a low voice. 'It's all too . . .'

'You don't have to say anything. It's all right.' He opened the door wider, allowing her to walk into the room, then locked it again. When he turned to Christine she was standing in the centre of the room with her back to him, shoulder sagging. He went to her and – somehow knowing right from wrong – picked her up in his arms and placed her gently on the bed. Her gaze remained fixed on him as he brushed traces of cigarette ash from her blouse and slacks, then lay down beside her, cradling her head in his left arm. He kissed her once, very lightly, asexually, before lowering his head on to the pillow. She slid her knee forward to rest on his thigh, and a stillness descended on the room.

Fifteen minutes left.

Christine raised her head to look at him, and now he found it difficult to see any trace of hardness in her face. 'I never told you,'

134

she said. 'My son died just before he was born. It was at a construction camp on Newhome. The doctor was away. I could feel the baby dying, but I couldn't help him. He was right there inside me, and there was nothing I could do to help him.'

'I'm sorry.'

'Thanks. I never tell anybody, you see. I was never able to talk about it.'

'It wasn't your fault, Chris.' He drew her head back down on to his shoulder.

'If I'd only stayed at home. If I'd only waited for Martin at home.'

'You weren't to know.' Surgenor uttered the age-old commonplace, the ritual absolution, with no trace of embarrassment, in the full understanding that the uniqueness of every human being and every human circumstance infused the words with new meaning. 'Try not to think about it.'

Don't sadden yourself by dwelling on past misfortunes, he thought. *Not now.*

Ten minutes left.

'Martin never forgave me. He died in a tunnel collapse, but that was four years after we'd split up. So I told you a lie this morning, Dave. I didn't have a husband who died – he dumped me because of what I'd done, then he died years later. On his own. Unilaterally, you might say.'

This morning? Surgenor was momentarily baffled. *What's she talking about?* He cast his mind back over recent events and felt a dull amazement when he realized that less than a day had elapsed since he had strolled out of the Service hostel on a blue-domed, glitter-bright morning – on a planet which was thirty million light-years away. *I'm caught in a squeeze play – between macro and micro. And what happens when the diameter of my pupils is less than the wavelength of light?*

Five minutes left.

'You wouldn't have done that, would you, Dave? You wouldn't have handed me all the blame.'

'There's no blame Chris – believe me.' To prevent the words being nothing more than words, Surgenor tightened his arm around Christine and felt her move in closer against him. *It's not as bad as it was,* he thought in wonderment. *It helps when you have somebody . . .*

No minutes left.
No seconds.
No time at all.

The first sound in the new existence was a chiming of bells.

It was followed by Aesop's voice making a general announcement. '. . . there is nothing outside. The ship and all its systems are undamaged, but there is nothing outside. There are no stars, no galaxies, no detectable radiation of any kind – nothing but blackness.

'It appears that we have an entire continuum to ourselves.'

eighteen

Surgenor found himself running towards the observation room.

He felt an unutterable gladness at still being alive against all the odds, but the feeling was counterbalanced by a new kind of dread – not fully acknowledged as yet – and it seemed imperative that he should scan the universe with his own eyes. Two men, Mossbake and Kessler, were swaying drunkenly outside the observation room door, their expressions a mixture of bleary triumph and surprise. Surgenor brushed past them and walked on to the gallery-like viewing area. The surrounding blackness was complete. He looked into it, absorbing the psychic punishment, then lowered himself into a chair beside Al Gillespie.

'It took no time at all,' Gillespie said. 'The sky looked the same right up to the last second. Then I got a feeling the stars were changing colours – then there was this. Nothing!'

Surgenor stared into the ocean of unrelieved night, his eyes darting here and there, uncontrollably, as his optic nerves registered spurious glimmers of light, creating and immediately destroying distant galaxies. Only by an effort of will was he able to prevent himself from shaking his head in denial.

'It looks as though conservation is conserved,' Gillespie said, almost to himself. 'Matter and energy aren't wasted. Go down a black hole – come up through a white hole. Go down a dwindlar – and you get a continuum to yourself.'

'We've only got Aesop's word for that. Where are the suns that must have come through before us?'

'Don't look at me, friend.'

'Hear these words, Aesop,' Surgenor said. 'How do you know all your receptors and pick-ups are functioning properly?'

'I know because my triplex monitoring circuits tell me so,' Aesop replied gently.

'Triplication doesn't mean a thing if each circuit has been given the same treatment.'

'David, you are venturing opinions on a highly specialized subject – one in which, according to your personal dossier, you have no qualifications or experience.' The computer's choice of words turned a statement of fact into a reproof.

'When it comes to going through a dwindlar,' Surgenor said doggedly, 'I have as much experience as you, Aesop. And I want access to the direct vision ports.'

'I have no objections to that,' Aesop replied, 'even though the request is unusual.'

'Good!' Surgenor got to his feet and glanced down at Gillespie. 'You coming?'

Gillespie nodded and stood up, and the two men left the observation room. On the way upstairs past the living quarters they were joined by Mike Targett, who seemed to sense where they were going. They reached the first of the computer decks, where the geognostic data banks occupied rows of metal cabinets, then climbed a little-used stair leading towards Aesop's central processing units.

Massive vacuum-tight doors slid aside to admit them to a circular gallery which skirted a forest of multicoloured cables, the enormously complex spinal cord which connected the *Sarafand*'s brain to its body. The computer itself still lay above them, beyond hatches which could be opened only by base maintenance teams. At four equidistant points around the gallery were circular ports which permitted direct vision of the ship's environment. Spaceship designers had a powerful aversion to putting holes in pressure shells, and in the case of the Mark Six they had grudgingly provided four small

137

transparencies in a part of the ship which could be hermetically sealed off from the other levels.

Surgenor went to the nearest port, looked through it and saw nothing but a man's face peering at him. He eyed the reflection for a moment, vainly trying to see through it, then asked Aesop to cut the interior lights. An instant later the deck was plunged into darkness. Surgenor looked out of the circular window, and the blackness was like an enemy lying in wait.

'There's nothing out there,' Targett whispered, from his position at another port. 'It's like we're sunk in pitch.'

'I can assure you,' Aesop said, speaking unexpectedly, 'that the surrounding medium is more transparent than interstella space. The amount of matter per cubic metre is precisely zero. Under these conditions my telescopes could detect a galaxy at a range of billions of light-years – but there are no galaxies to detect.'

'Let's have the light again Aesop.' Surgenor resisted an impulse to apologize to the computer for having doubted its word. He was relieved when the glowtubes sprang into brightness once more, shuttering the portholes with reflections.

'Well, we're not dead – at least I think we're not – but this is worse than the last time,' Targett said. He held up his hands and examined them, frowning.

Gillespie looked at him curiously. 'Shakes?'

'No – not yet. One of the old classical philosophers – I think it was Kant – used to talk about a situation like this. He said, suppose there was nothing anywhere in the whole universe but one human hand – would you be able to state that it was a left hand or a right hand? His answer was that you would, and this proved to him that there was a handedness about space itself, but he was wrong. Later thinking brought into account the idea of rotation through four-space . . .'

Targett stopped speaking and his boyish face seemed to crease into age. 'Oh, Jesus – what are we going to *do*?'

'There's nothing we can do except sit tight,' Surgenor said. 'Ten minutes ago we thought we were finished.'

'This is different, Dave. No more outside factors. This time there's nothing left but ourselves.'

'That reminds me,' Gillespie said in a dour voice, 'we'd better call another meeting as soon as everybody sobers up.'

'Is it worth another meeting? That's all we seem to do – and it might be best if they went on being drunk.'

'That's the whole point. Liquor is food. It's loaded with calories, and it'll have to be rationed out like anything else.'

The meeting was fixed for ship midnight, which left Surgenor two hours in which to think about dying of starvation, dying of loneliness in an empty and black continuum, dying of spiritual hypothermia. He kept on the move, rather than return to brood in his room, but this had the effect of indefinitely multiplying his sense of shock. A few minutes of involvement with some menial job would drive the hopelessness of the situation to the back of his mind, and then as the task was on the verge of completion an inner voice would tell him it was time to start thinking about the overall picture again, and he would take another mental plunge.

Once he encountered Christine Holmes in the corridor near his room and tried to speak to her, but she slipped past him with the impersonal gaze of a stranger and he understood that neither of them had anything to give or receive. He continued moving, working, talking, and was confronted when the designated hour arrived and the eleven remaining members of the *Sarafand*'s company drew together at the long table in the mess. The 'windows' around the semi-circular outer wall were dark, as befitted the middle of the night, but the room lights glowing orange and yellow and white created an atmosphere of secure warmth.

Just as the meeting was about to begin, Gillespie took Surgenor aside. 'Dave, how about if I do the talking for a change?'

'Suits me.' Surgenor smiled at Gillespie, suddenly appreciative of the fact that the former Idaho foodstuffs salesman had acquired new stature. 'I'll back you up this time.'

Gillespie went to the head of the table and stood there until the others had taken their seats. 'I guess I don't need to tell anybody here that we've run into big trouble. It's so big that none of us can see a way out – even Captain Aesop can't see a way out – but, just the way we did when we thought we could reach a planet, we're going to agree a set of rules. And we're going to stick to them for as long as it takes.'

'Dress for dinner, stiff upper lip, salute the Queen,' Burt Schilling muttered. He had swallowed two Antox capsules, but his face had a

139

sullen stiffness about it which suggested that he was still drunk.

'Most of the rules will, of course, be concerned with how we make use of our supply of food,' Gillespie said, unperturbed, glancing at his note pad. 'I think we want to prolong life – but not beyond a reasonable period, not under conditions which would make it mean-ingless – and for that reason it is proposed that we have a daily ration of a thousand calories of solid food and non-alcoholic beverages for each person. Aesop has supplied me with an inventory, and on the basis of a thousand calories each per day we have enough food to last eighty-four days.'

We'll be old by then, Surgenor thought. *It isn't a long time, but getting through it will wear us down to nothing.*

'We'll be a lot thinner, naturally enough, but Aesop says a proper mix of protein, fat and carbohydrate will keep us healthy.' Gillespie paused and looked around the table. 'Next there's the question of booze – which isn't so easy to decide. Taken over the same period of eighty-four days, we have three hundred calories a day each in beer and wine, and two-forty calories a day in spirits. The thing we have to work out is do we in fact want a daily ration, or would it be better to save it for a . . .?'

'I'm sick of listening to all this crap,' Schilling announced, slap-ping the table. We don't have to make rules and regulations about how we drink.'

Gillespie remained calm. 'The food and drink has to be properly allocated.'

'Not as far as I'm concerned,' Schilling said. 'I'm not going to sit around here nibbling crusts for the next three months. I don't want *any* food – I'll take my ration in booze. All of it in booze.'

'You can't do that.'

'Why not?' Schilling tried to sound reasonable. 'It would mean extra solid food for the ones that like that sort of stuff.'

Gillespie placed his note pad on the table and leaned towards him. 'Because you could pour your entire ration down your throat in a couple of weeks, *easily*; then when you sobered up you'd decide you weren't ready to starve just yet, and other people would have to feed you. That's why not.'

Schilling snorted. 'All right, all right. I'll make private deals with my friends – my food for their liquor.'

'We're not going to permit that sort of thing, either,' Gillespie said. 'It would lead to the same situation.'

Listening to the exchange, Surgenor was in general agreement with Gillespie, and yet he felt that some degree of flexibility was required. He was wondering how to voice his opinion without appearing to go against Gillespie when Wilbur Desanto – who had begun to partner Gillespie in *Module Two* – raised his hand.

'Excuse me, Al,' Desanto said unhappily. 'All these calculations are based on eleven people being around for the whole period – but what if anybody wants to get it over with right now?'

'You mean commit suicide?' Gillespie considered the idea for a moment and shook his head. 'Nobody would want to do that.'

'Wouldn't they?' Desanto gave the others at the table a lop-sided, shame-faced smile. 'Maybe Billy Narvik had the right idea.'

'Narvik tripped and fell by accident.'

'You weren't there,' Schilling put in. 'He did the neatest swallow dive I've seen in years. He *meant* to do it, man.'

Gillespie puffed out his cheeks impatiently. 'Narvik is the only one who can settle this argument, so if you see his ghost coming out of the tool store let me know, will you?' He studied the faces at the table, making sure his sarcasm had not been wasted. 'And until that happens I'd like to concentrate on the living. Okay?'

Desanto raised his hand again. 'How about it, Al? What's the arrangement for anybody who decides he'd rather have a quick exit? Will Aesop issue the right sort of package in the dispensary?'

'For the last time ...'

'It's a legitimate query,' Surgenor said in a low voice. 'I think it deserves some sort of an answer.'

Gillespie looked betrayed. 'For starters, Aesop doesn't carry suitable drugs in his inventory. He's programmed to jump back to the nearest Service base if any crewman develops a serious illness, so ...'

'That's it!' Victor Voysey spread his hands in a QED gesture. 'Somebody should pop an appendix, and Aesop will just *have* to get us back home.'

'In any case,' Gillespie continued, ignoring the interruption, 'Aesop wouldn't assist a man to end his own life, no matter what the circumstances were.'

141

'Let's ask him about that – just to make sure.'

'*No!*' Gillespie's voice was hard. 'The purpose of this meeting is to discuss arrangements for staying alive. Anybody who wants to talk to Aesop about how to commit suicide can do it privately in his room later on, but it seems to me that any moron should be able to arrange a simple little thing like that without any help from a lousy computer. It seems to me that it doesn't take much imagination, and that anybody who really wanted to kill himself could easily do it without making grandstand plays at our general meetings and wasting everybody else's time.'

'Thank you, Al.' Desanto stood up and gave a curious little bow. 'I apologize for wasting everybody's valuable time.' He pushed his chair back, walked to the companionway and climbed up it to the sleeping quarters, nodding thoughtfully to himself.

'Somebody should go after him,' Mossbake said nervously.

'There's no need,' Gillespie countermanded. 'Wilbur couldn't commit suicide to save his life. I know him – he's gone a bit huffy 'cause I told him off.'

The meeting resumed with a distinctly different atmosphere from that which had been prevalent in the initial stages, even the mulish Schilling going along with its general resolutions. Surgenor, in spite of his unvoiced reservations, had to admit that Gillespie's bluff organizational approach had provided a steadying influence. He was doing what Surgenor had so often done in the past – stepping into the command vacuum, making himself into a tangible and identifiable target for the negative emotions human beings always experienced when things were going wrong.

It was a courageous thing to do under the circumstances, Surgenor decided. The ship was a tiny bubble of light and heat, surrounded by black infinities of emptiness, and there were no prospects other than that things would continue to go further and further wrong until the captain and all his jolly sailor boys were dead. A lot of negative emotions were going to be generated before the end . . .

'I think we've done enough for one day,' Gillespie said an hour later, glancing at his watch. 'It's past one o'clock, and we could do with a break.'

'Too right,' Kessler grumbled as the members of the group stood up and looked at each other uncertainly.

Gillespie gave an artificial-sounding cough. 'There's just one more thing – the liquor rationing scheme we agreed on only applies to the ship's official stores, not to private supplies. Enough said?'

There was an immediate flurry of excitement as men who had just been browbeaten into accepting austerity got the unexpected scent of a final mind-erasing, peace-bringing alcoholic feast. Those who had little or no personal reserves of intoxicants looked hopefully at the known stockists and began crowding round them with offers of cigars and home-baked cakes without which, they claimed, no party would be a success. The easing of tension, coupled with the knowledge that their respite would be brief, precipitated the younger men like Rizno and Mossbake into noisy horseplay.

'Nice touch,' Surgenor murmured to Gillespie. 'There's nothing like a Mardi Gras hangover to make Lent seem like a good idea.'

Gillespie nodded looking gratified. 'I've got a bottle of cognac in my room. What do you say the two of us go up there and split it?'

Surgenor nodded, his gaze drawn to Christine Holmes, who had separated from the others and was making her way upstairs. Suddenly realizing where she was going, he excused himself and hurried after her. He went up the steps two at a time, entered the corridor and found Christine standing hesitantly outside No. 4, Wilbur Desanto's room. She was listening intently.

'I knocked a couple of times,' she said as Surgenor halted beside her. 'He doesn't answer.'

Surgenor reached past her and threw the door open. The room was almost in darkness, the only light coming from a printed page which was projected on to the ceiling from a micro-reader beside the bed. Desanto was stretched out on the bed, unmoving, his face turned towards the wall. Surgenor switched on the main light, and Desanto raised himself on one elbow, smiling his lop-sided smile.

'What do you guys want?' he said. 'Is the meeting over?'

'Why didn't you answer when I knocked?' Christine demanded over Surgenor's shoulder.

'Guess I must have dozed off. What's all the fuss about anyway?'

'There's a bottle party starting downstairs – thought you'd like to know.' Surgenor closed the door and stood looking down at Christine, whose face had hardened with anger.

'I swear he did that on purpose,' she said in a taut whisper, 'and I fell for it.'

143

'There's no need to put it that way – you didn't fall for anything.' Surgenor felt he was taking a risk, but he pressed ahead. 'You thought he might be trying to kill himself, and you were worried about it even though you hardly know him. That's good, Chris. It shows . . .'

'That I'm still human? In spite of everything?' Christine almost smiled as she reached for her cigarettes. 'Do me a favour, big Dave – forget that I went to your room. Deathbed recantations aren't worth a damn.'

Surgenor glanced to his left as he heard Gillespie ascending the steps. 'Al and I are going to open a bottle of his fancy brandy. Would . . .'

'There'll be more fun downstairs.' She walked away from him, brushed past Gillespie and clattered down the companionway, expertly transferring most of her weight to the handrail by way of her forearms to make a sliding descent.

'You trying to get something going there?' Gillespie said, giving Surgenor a quizzical look.

'What are you talking about?' Surgenor was reminded of the meaningful stare Billy Narvik had directed at him after their tussle a few paces along the same corridor, and he became indignant. 'What are you saying, Al? Does she look my type?'

'She doesn't look anybody's type, but there's nothing else available around here.'

'Chris puts on a show, you know. She's been churned up a few times and she doesn't want to risk it happening again, so she . . .' Surgenor abandoned what he had been going to say as he saw Gillespie's eyebrows creeping up. 'Why are we standing around here? Are we aging the booze?'

They went into Gillespie's room, which was next to Desanto's, and Gillespie produced two glasses and a resplendent bottle of pot-distilled brandy. 'This was supposed to give me one shot a night for a thirty-day mission, but I'm ready to see it off tonight and forget the gracious living bit.'

'You'll forget everything.'

'So?'

'So . . .' Surgenor held out his glass and watched its transformation into an orb of sunlight. 'Here's to amnesia.'

'Long may she reign.'

144

The two men sat in companionable quietness, drinking slowly but steadily, savouring the escape from reality. Surgenor's warmest memories of life in the Service were of lengthy bull sessions, which sometimes went on all night, while the ship was circling an alien star and its crew were drawn together by enhanced awareness of their humanity. Here the effect was greater. Having been buffeted by the tides and maelstroms of space, the ship was now becalmed in a boundless black sea. An infinity of emptiness pressed inwards on its shell, and all those on board knew the adventuring was over, because in a continuum where nothing existed nothing could happen. No surprises lay in store, except for those unexpected discoveries a human being may make about himself, and therefore the only logical thing to do was to concentrate on being human, extra-human, more than human. Tomorrow that would be difficult because the countdown to death would have begun, but for the time being . . .

'Albert Gillespie and David Surgenor!' Aesop's voice jolted Surgenor out of his drowsiness. 'Please acknowledge that you can hear me.'

Taking his cue from the fact that his name had been mentioned first, Gillespie said, 'Hear these words, Aesop – we're listening to you.' His eyes were wide with speculation as he set down his glass and glanced at Surgenor.

'The unusual circumstances in which we find ourselves have brought about some changes in my relationship with crew members,' Aesop said. 'As Michael Targett had already observed, I am simply a computer and my areas of competence are necessarily limited by the characteristics of my programmes. This is an in-built limitation brought about – as we have discovered – by the programmers' inability to foresee every possible type of situation. Do you understand what I am saying?'

'That's quite clear.' Gillespie jerked into an upright position. 'Aesop, are you saying you might have made a mistake about what's outside the ship?'

'Not about what is outside – but an internal event is taking place which I am unable to explain and which appears to transcend all my frames of reference.'

'Aesop, don't waffle about,' Surgenor chipped in. 'What's happening? Why did you call us?'

'Before I describe the phenomenon, I wish to clarify the position with regard to inter-crew relationships. In normal circumstances I make important announcements to all crew members simultaneously, but I have no way to estimate or judge the psychological effects of what I have to say, and I fear they may be harmful. You two have assumed positions of responsibility – do you accept the further responsibility of transmitting my message in what you deem to be a suitable form to the other nine members of the ship's company?'

'We do,' Surgenor and Gillespie said together. Surgenor, his heart beginning to lurch, cursed Aesop's inhuman tendency to wordiness.

'Your acceptance is noted,' Aesop said, and there followed a delay which intensified Surgenor's unease.

'Aesop, will you please get on with . . .'

'Albert, at 00.09 hours this morning, during the general meeting of the ship's company, you uttered the following words with respect to the deceased crewman William Narvik – "If you see his ghost coming out of the tool room store let me know." Do you remember saying that?'

'Of course I remember it,' Gillespie said, 'but it was only a joke, for God's sake. You've heard us making jokes before this, Aesop.'

'I am familiar with all the various tropes associated with humour. I am also familiar with various writings of a religious, metaphysical and superstitious nature which describe a ghost as resembling a patch of white, misty radiance.' Aesop's voice was calm, inflexible.

'And I must inform you that an object which has the classical attributes of a ghost is now emerging from the corpse of William Narvik.'

'Bull,' Surgenor said, and he repeated the word to himself numerous times as he and Gillespie made their way downstairs, quietly crossed the mess room and went down the wider stair which led to the hangar deck. He was still intoning it when the door of the tool store slid open at Aesop's command and they saw – enveloping Billy Narvik's torso and expanding outwards from it – a lens-shaped cloud of cold, white brilliance.

nineteen

Surgenor was surprised to discover – after the passing of a single, unmanning spasm of alarm – that he was unafraid.

He advanced into the tool store with Gillespie and saw that what he had taken to be a simple hemisphere of light was, in fact, complex in its topography and had traces of an internal structure. Its surface was ill-defined, rendering the curvatures more bewildering to the eye, and the regions of varying density within overlapped and shone through each other in a way which made it difficult for Surgenor to focus on individual features.

The object was about a metre in diameter, a dome of icy luminance shrouding most of Narvik's body. As he looked at it from close quarters Surgenor developed a conviction that he was seeing only half of a spheroid, that an equal amount of it curved downwards through the floor and the underlying supports. Obeying his instinct, he knelt down, extended one hand and briefly passed it through the glowing surface. There was no sensation of any kind.

'It's getting bigger,' Gillespie said. He took a step backwards and pointed at the nearer rim, which was silently spreading across the metal floor. In the space of a few seconds Narvik's head was entirely lost to view beneath the intangible shell of light. The two men linked hands like small children and backed to the door, their eyes white with reflection, minds brimming with wonder – and in the centre of the room the enigmatic hemisphere continued its growth at a visibly increasing pace.

'What is it?' Gillespie whispered. 'It looks like a brain, but . . .'

Surgenor felt his mouth go dry as the fear he should have experienced earlier stirred within him. Its source lay not in the awesome strangeness of the shining object, but – incredibly – in his slow-dawning sense of recognition. With an effort he managed to focus his eyes on a single part of the cloud, instead of taking it in as a whole, and thought he could see the beginnings of corpuscularity. As the object grew larger its structure was showing discontinuity, revealing itself to be composed of millions of motes of light.

'Hear these words, Aesop,' he said, forcing the speech sounds into existence. 'Can you get a microscope on to that thing?'

'Not yet – my diagnostic microscopes are limited in traverse to the main floor area of the hangar,' Aesop replied. 'But at its present rate of progress the object will penetrate the tool store wall in approximately two minutes, and I will then be able to subject it to high magnification.'

'Penetrate?' Surgenor recalled his idea that they could see only half of the luminous entity. 'Aesop, how about the engine bays below us – can you see anything unusual in there?'

'I am unable to see directly into the box columns of the spine, but there is a light source there. The implication is that the object extends downwards through the floor of the tool store.'

'What's going on?' Gillespie said, his gaze hunting over Surgenor's face. 'Do you know what that thing is?'

'Don't you?' Surgenor gave a numb, uncertain smile as he stared into the spreading billows of light. 'That's the universe, Al. You're looking at the whole of creation.'

Gillespie's jaw sagged, then he moved away, symbolically dissociating himself from Surgenor's statement. 'You're crazy, Dave.'

'Think so? Watch that screen.'

The glowing cloud had reached the limits of the circular tool room and now was expanding into the hangar area, spilling through the metal walls as though they had no objective reality. There were a number of furtive movements in the overhead beams as Aesop's long-range microscopes, normally used for inspecting faults in the survey modules, swung into new positions. At the same instant the monitoring screens came to life with the sort of images Surgenor had never expected to see on them – deep, dark and dizzy perspectives of thousands of lenticular galaxies in flight, moving, swarming, coming into focus and blurring out of it. The impression was that millions of years of observation through a powerful telescope had been compressed into a short film – a film designed to ensnare the mind and chasten the soul of any intelligent being who watched it. Surgenor strove to come to terms with the reality behind the words he had so glibly uttered a minute earlier.

Gillespie staggered a little, pressing both hands to his temples, as the blizzard of galaxies went on and on.

'Mike Targett should be down here to watch this,' Surgenor said, partly to himself. 'We're still in the grip of his dwindlar, you see. It's a cyclic process – just like the universe itself. It shrank us to nothing, and then – because conservation is conserved – something happened ... the stresses were relieved, or the signs were reversed ... the opposite to a balloon being blown up until it finally bursts ... and we went from micro to macro, from zero dimensions to the ultimate dimensions.'

'Dave!' There was a note of pleading in Gillespie's voice. 'Take it slower, will you?'

'That's the universe you see pouring out across the floor, Al, but it isn't really getting any bigger – it's maintaining its own natural size and we're contracting back into it. Right now the *Sarafand* is maybe a thousand times bigger than the universe, but soon it'll be the same size as the universe, then we'll shrink down through all the galaxies that make up the universe, then we'll be the size of a single galaxy, then of a single star system, then we'll get back to normal, but only for an instant, because we'll be back in the dwindlar zone, and we'll keep on shrinking till we get to zero – *and then the whole process will start over again*!'

There was the sound of heavy footsteps on metal and Sig Carlen appeared on the stair with a beer glass in his hand. 'Why don't you two characters stop being so ... What's *that*?'

Surgenor looked at the cloud of brilliant specks, the perimeter of which was now advancing across the hangar at walking pace, and then at Gillespie. 'You tell him, Al – I want to hear somebody else saying it.'

By the time the *Sarafand*'s crew had assembled in the mess room, and had sobered up with the aid of Antox capsules, the universe was larger than the ship.

A continuous rain of galaxies was spraying up through the floor, passing through the table and chairs and human beings, and out through the ceiling into the vessel's upper levels. The galaxies looked like slightly fuzzy stars to the naked eye, but when examined with a magnifying glass they were seen to be perface little lens-shapes or spirals, miniature jewels being squandered into space by an insane creature.

Surgenor sat at the long table, bemused, watching the motes of light pass through his own arms and hands, and tried to comprehend that each one contained a hundred million suns or more, and that vast numbers of those suns were the hearth-fires of civilizations. A reaction had set in after his first flash of inspirational understanding, and now – as with a picture in which hollows can also be seen as hills – his perceptions kept rebounding between two extremes. In one second he would be a normal-sized man watching specks of fire magically penetrating his flesh without hurting him; in the next he was a giant of inconceivable proportions, whose body was larger than the volume of space known to Earth's astronomers ...

'... can't take this in,' Theo Mossbake was saying. 'If it's all true, it means that the ship and our bodies have been converted into the most diffuse gas imaginable – one atom every million light-years or so. I mean, we ought to be *dead*.'

'Forget everything you learned at school,' Mike Targett replied. 'We're dealing with dwindlar physics now, and all the rules are different.'

'I still don't see why we aren't dead.'

Targett, who had been the first to grasp the dwindlar's concept, spoke with evangelical fervour. 'I tell you, Theo, it's all different. if you think about it, the laws of conventional science say we should have died when we shrank. We should have become so dense that we turned into a micro neutron star – but we didn't. Perhaps the atoms themselves, and the particles they're made from, were reduced in proportion in some way. I don't know how it worked – but I do know that we're now at the opposite end of the scale.'

Voysey clicked his fingers. 'If we're going to shrink down through our original size, does that mean that Aesop will be able to operate the ship's drive again?'

'Afraid not,' Targett said. 'Aesop will correct me on this if I'm wrong, but it takes many minutes for him to prepare and carry out a beta-space jump – and we'll pass through our original size in some fantastically small fraction of a second. You can see the way the process is speeding up. Those galaxies are farther apart and travelling faster than they were when we sat down here. As they appear to get bigger they'll keep on speeding up, and soon they'll be moving so fast we won't be able to see them.'

Targett paused to watch the upward migration of fireflies. 'In fact, as far as we're concerned, they'll eventually have to travel thousands, millions of times faster than light – but that's because we'll be contracting at that speed. It's a weird thought.'

'Talking about weird thoughts,' Christine Holmes said in a small voice, making her first contribution to the discussion, 'I keep thinking of what Dave and Al told us about Billy Narvik's body and the light coming out through it. Why did it start there, of all places?'

'Pure coincidence, Chris. Dave dragged the body into the tool store and laid it on the ship's centre of gravity marker plate – and the centre of gravity is the one invariant point in the whole set-up. It must still be occupying its original position in the universe, and the ship is condensing towards it equally from all directions. That's why we're going to end up in the dwindlar zone again, and not in some other part of ... of the ...'

Targett's voice faltered and his face grew visibly paler as he turned to Surgenor. 'The centre of gravity, Dave – we can shift it.'

'Enough?' Surgenor stared back at him through a spray of galaxies. 'The equivalent of thirty million light-years?'

'That's the width of a little finger – we're big boys now, Dave.' Targett smiled the thin, cool smile of a man who has transcended his mortal destiny. 'The calculations should be easy for Aesop, and even if we miss our chance on this cycle, we can try again next time round.'

Four days later, the survey ship *Sarafand* – having once again engulfed the entire universe and imploded back into it – materialized in normal-space near a yellow sun. After a brief pause it began its slow, patient approach to the landing field in Bay City, on the planet called Delos.

twenty

'Hear these words, Aesop,' Surgenor said. He had finished packing his belongings into his single woven-glass travelling case, and was ready to quit the room which had been his only permanent home for almost twenty years. The room was small and plain, little more than a metal box equipped with a few basic amenities, but at the last moment he felt reluctant to leave.

'I'm listening to you, Dave.' Aesop's voice seemed louder than usual, due to the quietness of the ship.

'I ... This is probably the last time I'll be speaking to you.'

'As you are about to leave the ship, and I am due to be decommissioned in sixteen minutes from now, it is certainly the last time you will be speaking to me. What do you want?'

'Well ...' Surgenor considered the utter stupidity of saying goodbye to a computer or asking it how it felt about its imminent death. 'I think I just wanted to see if you were still functioning.'

There was a protracted silence, then Surgenor realized that Aesop – having demonstrated that he was still fully operative – considered that no further words were necessary. *It's only logical*, Surgenor thought, picking up his case. He left the room, walked along the bow-shaped corridor and went down the companionway into the empty mess. Extra tables had been set up in it, and they were still littered with empty glasses and plates left over from the morning's Press reception. A half-smoked cigar had been trodden into the floor and Surgenor kicked it out of his way as he went to the stair and proceeded down it to the hangar deck.

For public safety reasons, a ring of red-painted stanchions linked by white rope had been set up around the gaping hole which he and the others had burned through the deck. Part of the tool store wall had been cut away too, the heat-rippled metal testifying to the speed at which the work had been carried out. Surgenor stared down into the darkness of the exposed engine bays, thinking about the hours of frantic, concerted activity which had wreaked so much havoc on the *Sarafand*'s structure.

The slicing of the heavy plates and beams had been necessary for two reasons. One requirement was that of giving Aesop's long-range microscopes an unimpeded view of the imaginary point which was the ship's centre of gravity, and which also corresponded with its original location in the universe. The other requirement was for extra masses of material which could be moved quickly and conveniently to one side of the hangar deck, thus changing – however minutely – the centre of gravity of the entire ship. Most of the mass shifting, however, had been done by driving two of the survey modules out of their stalls under Aesop's precise and precisely timed instructions.

Surgenor had little knowledge of advanced maths, but he had a feeling that Mike Targett – young hero of the hour – had been overly confident and now was overly complacent about what they had achieved. They had allowed the ship to complete the dwindlar's contraction–expansion cycle once to give Aesop a practice run at orienting himself among the profusion of galaxies which made up the universe, and at performing the computations which would determine the new centre of gravity. This time, at the instant of reversal, they had known not to look outside the ship, but had instead congregated around the tool store and had seen a point of searing brilliance – the universe – springing into existence on the cross-hairs which had been rigged up at the centre of the gaping hole.

The awe Surgenor had experienced at that moment returned to him, reinforcing his conviction that the *Sarafand* and its crew had, in the last extremity, been lucky. They had been caught in a dangerous mathematical pincer movement. So massive was the ship that it had been possible to shift its centre of gravity only by a scant two centimetres on the normal scale of size – but at one stage in the dwindlar cycle this would have been enough to deposit them a hundred times farther from their home galaxy than the original thirty million light-years they had been unable to cross. And at a later stage it would simply have dropped them into a different region of the same alien galaxy, or even back into the edge of the dwindlar zone itself. With little more than instinct to go on, Surgenor was left with a feeling that – despite the fantastic powers of Aesop's processing units – the outcome could have been disastrous.

He shrugged his shoulders, ridding himself of an invisible burden, crossed to the hangar deck entrance and walked down the long ramp to a familiar sunlit field. In twenty years he had driven down that same ramp hundreds of times, with the horizons of an unknown planet rising to enfold him, yet on this occasion the sense of strangeness was greater. He had a fair idea of what lay ahead – and the unknown quantity was within himself. He had retired from the Service, and because of the special circumstances was being allowed out almost at once, which faced him with the problem of not having any problems, of having to live as other men lived, of no longer being a wilful stranger . . .

'Hi, Dave!' Al Gillespie was meticulously polishing the windshield of a rented car, and he looked up at Surgenor with a smile. 'Do you want a ride into town?'

'Thanks, but I'd rather walk.' Surgenor shaded his eyes from the sun and scanned a range of blue hills that lay to the east. 'I'm going to start walking to the places I want to reach.'

'You'll soon get tired of that.'

'Think so?'

Gillespie gave the car a final unnecessary dab. 'I'll bet on it. Remember all that stuff the Commissioner said on TV this morning about universe ships designed with special big movable weights inside them? The ones he said will deliberately head for the dwindlar to give science teams a proper look at the universe? I'll bet that when they've got one built you'll volunteer for the trip.'

Surgenor felt a touch of coldness along his spine, but it faded immediately and he smiled. 'You might be on that trip, Al – but I won't.'

'See you around, Dave,' Gillespie said knowingly. He lowered himself into the car and drove away in the direction of the distant administrative buildings, which glowed with pastel colours in the afternoon sunshine.

Surgenor watched him depart, then turned his attention to the mountainous hulk of the ship rising above him. Work had already begun on stripping off the four triangular fairings which housed part of the drive machinery. Mobile robocranes surrounded the *Sarafand*, like insects dismembering a much larger but helpless victim, and the air was filled with their hydraulic chirpings. Surgenor found the sight distasteful. He had hoped the ship would be preserved intact, perhaps as a museum piece, but that would have meant transporting it closer to the centre of the Bubble, and the Space Safety Board had declared it unfit to fly.

Feeling very much out of place amid the wrecking crews and the technicians who were ascending and descending the ramp, Surgenor loitered on the ferrocrete apron until he saw what he had been waiting for – the tall, straight-backed figure of Christine Holmes emerging from the shadows of the hangar deck. He had seen very little of her in the crowded week that had passed since the touchdown on Delos, but he knew she had taken advantage of special rulings and was quitting the Service. She came down the ramp with a jaunty stride – cigarette angled between her lips, flight bag slung on her shoulder – looking competent and self-possessed, and he felt a sudden trepidation about what he had planned.

'Still here, Dave?' Christine paused beside him and inclined her head towards the nearest crane. 'You shouldn't watch this stuff, you know.'

'It doesn't bother me. Anyway, I was waiting for you.'

She narrowed her eyes in appraisal. 'Why?'

'Thought we might have a drink together.'

'Oh? Do you know any good spots?'

'Lots of them. On Earth.'

'Thanks for the offer, Dave – but no thanks.' She hitched the flight bag higher on her shoulder and stepped past him. 'I'm not as thirsty as I thought I was.'

Surgenor moved quickly to bar her way. 'It was a genuine offer, Chris, and at least it deserves a genuine answer.'

'I gave you one – no *is* an answer.' Christine sighed, dropped her cigarette and ground it under heel. 'Look, Dave, I'm not trying to be bitchy – I really do thank you for the offer – but isn't this a bit silly? Shipboard romances always fizzle out when you get to port, and when you have a shipboard *nothing* . . .'

Surgenor was aware of bystanders beginning to take an interest in the confrontation, but he pressed on. 'It wasn't a nothing when you came to my room that night.'

'Wasn't it?' Christine gave a sarcastic laugh. 'Don't tell me you took advantage when I was . . .'

'Don't talk to me that way,' Surgenor snapped, gripping her shoulders, determined to hurl his message across the gulf of lost years that separated their lives. 'I'll tell you what happened that night, and I know better because I'm a bigger expert on loneliness than you are. You were faced with something you didn't know how to handle alone, and you came to me for help. Now I'm faced with something I don't know how to handle alone, and . . .'

'And you're coming to me for help?'

'Yes.'

Christine caught hold of Surgenor's wrists and slowly disengaged his hands from her shoulders. 'You're crazy, big Dave.' She turned and walked away across the dusty ferrocrete.

'And you,' Surgenor called after her, 'are . . . *stupid*!'

Christine continued walking for perhaps ten paces, then halted and stared at the ground for a moment before walking back to him. 'You've some nerve calling me stupid – have you any idea what you'd be taking on if I went with you?'

'No, but I'm prepared to find out.' Surgenor strove for the right words, the best words. 'It'll be a new kind of trip for me.'

Christine hesitated, and he saw her lips were trembling. 'All right,' she said soberly. 'Let's go.'

Surgenor picked up his own case, and he and Christine – separated from each other by a short distance – walked towards the field's far-off perimeter. The sudden warmth of the sun on his back told Surgenor when he had emerged from the shadow of the ship, but he did not look back.

Bob Shaw
Who Goes Here? 75p

'One of the most impressive writers of the genre' SUNDAY TIMES

In the 24th century, men join the Space Legion to forget – a memory-erasing machine makes sure they do just that. The machine erases all traces of guilt, but for recruit Warren Peace it has wiped out everything. He must have a very nasty past indeed ... Into battle with the Legion, and Warren faces vicious predators in fearsome conflict without the slightest idea why he's been stupid enough to sign on in the first place!

'Very funny ... incidents run amok' THE TIMES

Arthur C. Clarke
The View from Serendip 90p

Speculations on Space, Science and the Sea, together with fragments of an Equatorial Autobiography.

'The film *2001* turned him into a cult figure ... His enthusiasm is so immense he finds it impossible to be dull ... his "continuing love affair" with Sri Lanka, his deep sea diving, his work on the film are as absorbing as anything he ever wrote'
COLIN WILSON, EVENING NEWS

'Gives voice to the romantic side of scientific enquiry'
NEW YORK TIMES

H. G. Wells
The War of the Worlds 70p

H. G. Wells' classic novel on the invasion of Planet Earth by warrior squadrons of an alien world – the undisputed masterpiece of science fiction. Now a CBS double album – Jeff Wayne's musical version, starring Richard Burton, Julie Covington, David Essex and more.

'Those who have never seen a living Martian can scarcely imagine the strange horror of their appearance ...'

Harlan Ellison
Deathbird Stories 80p

'The grimoires and *Necronomicons* of the gods of the freeway, of the ghetto blacks, of the coaxial cable; the paingod and the rock god and the god of neon ... the gods that live in city streets and slot machines. The God of Smog and the God of Freudian Guilt. The Machine God. Know them now ... they rule the nights through which we move' HARLAN ELLISON

'The chief prophet of the New Wave in science fiction' NEW YORKER

Richard Cowper
The Custodians 60p

'The Custodians': A room constructed at the intersection of mysterious force fields, so that anyone entering can foresee the future ... 'Paradise Beach': A wall-screen that attunes itself to the individual perceptions of the onlooker ... 'Piper at the Gates of Dawn': The magical tale of an old storyteller, an enchanted piper and a mysterious white bird ... 'The Hertford Manuscript': A 17th-century book that appears to be the journals of a 19th-century traveller ...

'Stories that should appeal even to the reader only mildly hooked on science fiction' EVENING STANDARD

Philip K. Dick
The Preserving Machine
and other stories 60p

'Fourteen of the best from this consistently entertaining writer, whose imagination is like those batteries that keep going long after the others have stopped' EVENING STANDARD

'The title story alone is almost worth the price in itself' DAILY TELEGRAPH

Michael Coney
Brontomek! 70p

The planet Arcadia is on the verge of economic collapse – its human colony decimated by the Relay Effect. The Hetherington Organization come up with an offer the Arcadians can't refuse – a plan to bring new prosperity to the planet.

But when the ships arrive, they unload a stream of Brontomeks – huge, armoured robot machines – and an army of amorphaliens, capable of moulding themselves into human form...

Christopher Priest
Inverted World 80p

Helward Mann leaves the City of Earth to become a Future Surveyor in an alien world – apparently familiar, but gradually revealing its strange difference. This world is 'inverted': a planet of infinite size existing in a finite universe...

'One of the most gifted and poetic young writers of science fiction' JOHN FOWLES

'One of the trickiest and most astonishing twist endings in modern SF' TRIBUNE

Indoctrinaire 75p

'A novelist of real distinction' THE TIMES

In a laboratory deep under the Antarctic, Wentik is experimenting with mind-affecting drugs. Suddenly he is transported into the 22nd-century Brazilian jungle. After nuclear war only South America has survived, but vestiges of the war gases remain to create 'The Disturbances' and threaten the social order. Wentik must return to his own time to find out about the gas and its antidote ... but finds himself in the wrong time-slot, and the War has already begun...

'Excellent ... a Kafka-type nightmare' SUNDAY TIMES

Alfred Bester
Starburst 60p

Eleven strange and startling stories from one of the most inventive authors in SF today, including 'Disappearing Act': A US Army hospital faces a problem – patients who disappear and reappear at will! 'Fondly Fahrenheit'; A killer robot and his master flee the planetary police ... 'The Roller Coaster': A girl from the future has a passionate affair with a twentieth-century man ... 'Adam and No Eve': The last man on Earth – sole survivor of a total, chain reaction holocaust.

'The pyrotechnic virtuoso of science fiction'
NEW YORK HERALD TRIBUNE

Robert Silverberg
Downward to the Earth 75p

The planet Belzagor is predominantly jungle, populated with bizarre flora and fauna, governed by the elephant-like alien *nildoror*, and the bi-pedal *sulidoror*. Gundersen was last on Belzagor when it was a colonial planet and he was an administrator; now he returns to meet old friends. But Gundersen is still driven by an old guilt, and he needs to undergo the bizarre *nildor* rite of 'rebirth' for his own metamorphosis ...

'Probably the most intelligent SF writer in America' URSULA LE GUIN